I0628461

THE FIREBRAND

A Comedy in the Romantic Spirit

THE FIREBRAND

A Comedy in the Romantic Spirit

BY

EDWIN JUSTUS MAYER

WILDSIDE PRESS

First Printing, December, 1924
Second Printing, February, 1925

NOTE

Although I have endeavored to retain the spirit of Cellini and of his times, as revealed in his autobiography, "The Firebrand" is inspirational rather than documental. I am indebted to Miss Marion Spitzer for her original suggestion to me that a play should be written about Cellini based on his love affair with one Angelica—whom I have called Angela and made his model in the comedy. In his rendition of this incident, Cellini relates that he fell in love with Angelica and that Beatrice, her mother, learning of his intention to steal the girl, fled with her. Some months later the artist heard from Angelica that she was in Sicily. "By that time I had beeen giving myself up to all the pleasures imaginable, and I had taken another love, but only to extinguish this earlier flame." Soon after, a murderous brawl made Cellini flee Rome; he sought refuge in Naples, and found Angela, "whose endearments to me were warmer than I can describe." Cellini struck a bargain with Beatrice, by which she surrendered her daughter. "Angelica begged me to buy her a gown of black velvet, which was very cheap in Naples. I did all they asked me willingly; sent for the velvet, bargained for and paid it; but the old woman, who thought me fatuously in love, demanded a gown of fine cloth for herself, would have had me lay out a great deal on her sons, and begged for more money than I had offered her. At this I turned to her good-naturedly and said. 'My dear Beatrice, didn't I offer you enough?' 'No,' she said. So I replied that what was not enough for her would suffice for me, and having kissed my Angelica, we parted, she with tears, I with a laugh. . . ."

THE FIREBRAND

As presented at the Morosco Theatre, New York,
on October 15, 1924

ASCANIO ....CHARLES McCARTHY
EMILIA ....HORTENSE ALDEN
BENVENUTO CELLINI ....JOSEPH SCHILDKRAUT
ANGELA ....EDEN GRAY
BEATRICE ....LILLIAN KINGSBURRY
PIER LANDI ....GEORGE DRURY HART
ALESSANDRO, Duke of Florence....FRANK MORGAN
OTTAVIANO, the Duke's Cousin....E. G. ROBINSON
POLVERINO ....ALLYN JOSLYN
THE DUCHESS ....NANA BRYANT
A SOLDIER ....WALLACE FORTUNE
A PAGE ....EDWARD QUINN

LADIES OF THE COURT ⎰ DOROTHY BICKNELL
⎱ ELEANOR EWING

GENTLEMEN OF THE COURT
AND SOLDIERS OF THE
DUCHY OF FLORENCE
⎰
Kenneth Dana
Robert Ploomer
Scott Hirschberg
Roland Winters
Philip Niblette
Oliver Hulton
Calvin Vollmer

THE FIREBRAND

CHARACTERS

ASCANIO, *Cellini's apprentice.*
EMILIA, *A servant.*
BENVENUTO CELLINI.
ANGELA, *Cellini's model.*
BEATRICE, *Her mother.*
PIER LANDI, *Cellini's friend.*
ALESSANDRO DE MEDICI, *Duke of Florence.*
OTTAVIANO DE MEDICI.
POLVERINO.
THE DUCHESS OF FLORENCE.
A SOLDIER.
A HANGMAN.
Courtiers, several ladies of the Duchess, Soldiers, a Page.

ACT I

Scene: Cellini's *workshop.* *Afternoon.*

ACT II

Scene I: *The garden of the Summer Palace, outside of Florence. Night.*
Scene II: *The balcony of the Palace. A few minutes later.*

ACT III

Scene: Cellini's *workshop. Late next morning.*

Time: **1535.**   Place: Florence.

THE FIREBRAND

ACT I

CELLINI'S *workshop in Florence. At the extreme right rear is the entrance from the street; the door is guarded by a heavy iron bolt, and several steps below it lead into the shop. To the left front is the large and ornamental door which leads into* CELLINI'S *house. Opposite this, right front, is a small door which leads into an adjunct of the shop. To the left rear is a small furnace with an anvil beside it. Behind the furnace and anvil is a Renaissance window, which floods the room with light. The ceiling is open above several beams, as though a little-used attic might be above. The shop itself is a hodge-podge of beauty made and in the making. Statues, both ancient and contemporary—the latter often unfinished—are littered about the room with various vases and exquisite curios. A table stands near the right front exit, with several chairs about it.*

ASCANIO, *a lad of perhaps seventeen, is busy hammering a mass of glowing metal on the anvil. He hums a tune in rhythm with his*

*swinging arm. A door is heard slamming out-
side left.* Ascanio, *as though guessing who
may be approaching, hides behind a pedestal
near the left front door just as it opens to
admit* Emilia, *the pretty serving wench of the
house, a year or two younger than the apprentice—who springs on her and kisses her savagely
before she is aware of his presence.*

EMILIA

[*Screaming and tearing herself loose, faces
    him.*]
You . . . you wolf! You bit me.

ASCANIO

[*Laughs.*]
Come here! Let me bite you again. You are
sweet to the taste.

EMILIA

[*Retreating from him.*]
Alligator! Crocodile! Vermin! You bit me.

ASCANIO

[*Trying to get at her.*]
I don't want to eat you. I want to love you.

EMILIA

[*With instinctive wisdom.*]
It's all the same with boys like you.

ASCANIO

[*Turning red.*]
I am not a boy.   I am a man.

EMILIA

[*Her chance to laugh.*]
MAN!   You are a boy—a bad boy.

ASCANIO

[*Very angry.*]
If you call me boy again, I'll do something worse
than bite you.   I'll—I'll smash your face!

EMILIA

[*Reveling in her new found power to enrage
    him.*]
Two-year-old!   Infant!   Diaper-giant!

ASCANIO

[*As she evades him.*]
Wait till I get hold of you.

EMILIA

[*Tauntingly.*]
You'll never get hold of me, boy.

ASCANIO

[*Picking up a chisel.*]
I'll make you wish you hadn't said that.   I'll cut
you up.

[Runs after her, but fearful of knocking over something precious, stops and glares.]

EMILIA

Cut me up! I said you would like to eat me, didn't I? And you said No.

ASCANIO

If you would be kind to me I would be kind to you.

EMILIA

I will never be kind to you.

ASCANIO

Then I will kick you until you are kind to me.

EMILIA

Kick me!

ASCANIO

[Perplexed at this himself.]
Only because I love you. . .

EMILIA

[Increasingly indignant.]
Kick me! So!—you learned that from your master.

ASCANIO

[Changing his pitch again.]
Don't you dare say anything against my master.

EMILIA

[*Impudently.*]
Why not?

ASCANIO

[*After a moment's thought.*]
He is a great man.

EMILIA

He is a great beast.

ASCANIO

[*Moving towards her once more.*]
Now I will certainly kick you.

EMILIA

[*Seizing the wax model of a vase which is near
her.*]
If you come any closer I will throw this to the
ground.

ASCANIO

[*In a panic.*]
Don't do that!

EMILIA

Then get out of my way.
[*She circles about him successfully until she is
in a direct line with the left front exit.*]

ASCANIO

[*In a sweat.*]

In the name of God, put that down! If you drop it, I will be beaten, I will be killed.

EMILIA

[*Still holding the vase.*]
You like to beat, but you do not like to be beaten.

ASCANIO

Only put it down and I will never touch you again! By all of the Saints!

EMILIA

[*Allowing his plea, gently.*]
Very well.   But remember your promise.

ASCANIO

[*Grimly, getting between her and the model.*]
I will . . . and also how you forced me to give it to you, Emilia.

EMILIA

[*With a wholly inexplicable change of demeanor; almost weeping.*]
I didn't want to hurt you. You made me do it.

ASCANIO

[*Ready to weep himself, at his mingled emotions of desire and humiliation.*]
You have made a fool of me.

EMILIA

No, no, Ascanio.

ASCANIO

You were right. I am only a boy. I am not a man.

EMILIA

[*Leaving the safety of the doorway and going to him.*]
I did not mean that, either. I never meant that.

ASCANIO

[*Turning away.*]
You said it.

EMILIA

[*Laying her hand on his shoulder.*]
We all say things we don't mean.

ASCANIO

[*Taking her hand.*]
I didn't mean that I would kick you, either.

EMILIA

[*Permitting him to retain her hand.*]
What did you mean?

ASCANIO

I meant that I loved you, that I wanted you, that I think of you when I work at day and in my bed by night!

EMILIA

[*Taking back her hand and covering her face.*]
Bed! . . . You mustn't say such things to me.

ASCANIO

[*Arrogant with the prescience of victory.*]
I will say to you—what I choose.

EMILIA

[*Stepping away rapidly.*]
No.

ASCANIO

[*Running after her.*]
Don't go.

EMILIA

[*Pausing.*]
I must go.

ASCANIO

I won't hurt you.

EMILIA

I am afraid.

ASCANIO

[*Catching her arm.*]
Let me kiss you . . . hug you. . . .

EMILIA

[*Shoving him from her.*]
No, no.

[*She runs out on him.* ASCANIO *returns glumly
to his work. But his thoughts, which at first
belong to* EMILIA, *are gradually absorbed by
the metal before him; and soon he begins to
hum again in rhythm with his blows. . . .*
CELLINI *bursts into the room, without warn-
ing, through the rear door, a large dagger in
his hand; in an instant, he has closed and
bolted the door and leans against it, breathing heavily.* CELLINI *is thirty-five and already his genius has made him celebrated.*]

CELLINI

[*With his whole heart.*]
Mother of God, the world is full of villains!
[ASCANIO *looks at him, full of curiosity, but contin-
ues to hammer away.* CELLINI *turns wrathfully.*]
Stop that infernal noise!

ASCANIO

[*Astounded.*]
But master, this is the cup for the Cardinal for
which he is in a hurry——

CELLINI

[*Struck by an idea.*]
The Cardinal!
[*He goes to the table, where there are writing
materials, and begins a note with intense*

earnestness. Ascanio, *looking from the anvil to his master, and back again, finally cannot longer contain himself.*]

ASCANIO

Master— [*Pause.*] Master——

CELLINI

[*Annoyed.*]
Shut up!

ASCANIO

[*Throwing himself at* CELLINI's *feet.*]
Master, forgive me, but the metal is just right and unless one of us goes on with it at once——

CELLINI

[*Examining the shining embryo.*]
So it is! Why have you stopped, you fool? Do you want me to lose the Cardinal's favor? Now, when I need all the influence I can muster?

ASCANIO

[*Appalled.*]
But, master, you told me to stop.

CELLINI

[*Indignant.*]
I? I? I? I told you to stop? Am I mad? Am I possessed? [*Folding the note.*] Ascanio, listen to

me. I must tell you that I am in great danger. I have just killed Maffio.

ASCANIO

[*Stunned.*]
Killed him?

CELLINI

Yes, I hung a bloody necklace around his throat which he will wear for a long time, I am happy to say.

ASCANIO

How—where was it?

CELLINI

Let me tell you all about it. [*He seats himself upon the table and begins his narrative with obvious enjoyment.*] I was coming home, through the narrow street, when I noticed a fellow standing on one side, and two on the other side. I thought, Benvenuto, you had better look out. Well, sure enough, as I came up, I saw that one was Maffio; when I knew that it was he, I was in a great heat to get at him, but seeing that the others would be at my back, I sprang to the wall and dared them to come on. You know how I am with a dagger; it is a family trait to handle one as Zeus handles the lightning! I turned away the two of them in a jiffy, and Maffio would have fled, but before he could do so, I struck him in the neck. Then I made off— [*He suddenly*

realizes that Ascanio *has begun to tap the cup again
and breaks off in disgust.*]   How often must I tell
you to stop making that damnable noise?

ASCANIO

[*Carried beyond fear by enthusiasm.*]
But, master, who could stop now? Why the thing
is anxious to be beaten into your design! [*Holds up
the spirited mass.*]   See! It cries out for its right
shape.

CELLINI

[*Approvingly.*]
By the Holy Church, I think you have actually
caught fire from me. You may make an artist yet.

ASCANIO

[*Abashed with pleasure.*]
But never an artist like you!

CELLINI

[*Dismissing the absurd idea.*]
Men like myself do not happen twice. But still,
you will be an artist [*regards the cup lovingly*] . . .
and that is a great thing. Do you know why? I
am in great danger of my life, at the moment,
Ascanio, but compared to other men who walk in
peace, I am a safe man. For all of us are born
naked, and we live in danger against the winds,
clothed only in the little safety we find which we call

beauty. This cup is a better armor to me than a pope's pardon: that vase is a visor which protects me from Time's battle-ax; and through that statue, I enter into the Holy Ghost before I die. Do you understand these things?

ASCANIO

[*Uncertainly.*]
I think that I do.

CELLINI

[*Mimicking his tone.*]
You think that you do! You are a great booby and will never be anything else. [*Handing him the note.*] Here, run with this to the Cardinal, and beg him intercede for me with the Duke. Tell him I was set upon by three men. I defended myself, and killed Maffio in the brawl. And here—take this vase as a gift from me—to the Cardinal—the ignorant fool will not appreciate it, but take it to him—and get back as quickly as you can. [ASCANIO *starts towards the rear door.*] No, that door stays shut. Go through the house. And send Angela to me. [ASCANIO *exits.* CELLINI *regards the cup with satisfaction.*] The idiot is not without talent.

    [ANGELA *enters. Since* CELLINI *uses her as his model, she is of course beautifully formed; and despite her experiences—brought on by her bawdy mother—she has retained a fine sweetness of expression.* CELLINI, *absorbed in his work, does not notice her until she speaks.*]

ANGELA

[*Timidly.*]
You sent for me?

CELLINI

[*Dropping his tools with delight.*]
Angela!

ANGELA

Shall I undress?

CELLINI

No, I will not work today.

ANGELA

But you wished to see me.

CELLINI

Must I see you only when I have a chisel in my hand? Do you never think that I am a man as well as an artist?

ANGELA

[*Confused.*]
My mother——

CELLINI

[*Spitting.*]
Do not mention that harridan!

ANGELA

[*Submissively.*]
Yes, Sir.

CELLINI

And do not say, Yes, Sir! It is my desire that
you call me Benvenuto.

ANGELA

[*Overawed by this condescension.*]
Yes, Sir.

CELLINI

Angela, my life is in the gravest danger.

ANGELA

[*With artless concern.*]
Oh, Sir, do not say that!

CELLINI

[*Harshly.*]
I have forbidden you to call me Sir. Let me hear
you call me Benvenuto.

ANGELA

[*In a soft tone.*]
Benvenuto.

CELLINI

Let me hear you say it again!

ANGELA

Benvenuto.

CELLINI

[*Throwing his arms wide in rapture.*]

Seraphs and nightingales! your songs are less than her common speech. Oh, Angela, Angela, I am a violent and dreadful man, covered with the blood of my enemies——

ANGELA

I had forgotten your danger.

CELLINI

[*Irritated.*]

Do not interrupt me, when I am speaking well.

ANGELA

[*Crushed.*]

I am sorry.

CELLINI

No, no, it is I who am sorry, for the music of your voice puts to shame the splendor of my words! I was born with a bird caged in my heart, and you have set the bird free, Angela.

ANGELA

[*Not knowing how to take this.*]

You are making fun of me.

CELLINI

I would as soon make fun of the Madonna! And

to think that you come into my life at its very
end. . .

ANGELA

Someone wishes to kill you?

CELLINI

A dozen men—but they fear me more than I fear
them. It is only the Duke's anger that I fear.

ANGELA

You have offended him?

CELLINI

I killed two men today, and I do not know what
he will do about it. When I was pardoned, it was
on condition that I keep the peace.

ANGELA

[*Scared.*]
Who was it you killed?

CELLINI

Maffio and another, whose name I don't know.
But let me tell you all about it. [*He adopts the
posture he had when telling* ASCANIO *the story, sitting on the table, and begins.*] I was coming home
through the narrow street, when I noticed three fellows standing on one side, and three on the other.
I thought, Benvenuto, you had better look out!
Well, sure enough, as I came up, I saw that one was

Maffio; when I saw that it was he, I was in a great heat to get at him, and sprang towards him; but a fellow getting in my way—and a huge fellow he was, with his dagger aimed straight for my heart—I turned aside his blow, and stabbed him where he would have stabbed me. (I must tell you that we Cellinis have been famous with sword and dagger for centuries.) Well, then I fought my way through the five of them, until I reached Maffio, the rest running away as fast as their accursed legs would carry them. Maffio would have gone with them, but I caught him and stabbed him, the blade going so deep that I had trouble withdrawing it.

ANGELA

[*Clasping her hands.*]
God save you!

CELLINI

Although I only defended myself, my enemies will make plenty out of the matter, and I shall probably be hanged.

ANGELA

[*Simply and sincerely.*]
When you say that, I could cry.

CELLINI

[*Gratified that his words have had their desired effect.*]
And if I am hanged, how long will you cry?

ANGELA

All of the day, unless my mother beats me and makes me stop.

CELLINI

[*Going to the door left front, and shouting.*]
If that beastly witch hits you again, I will break every bone in her body!—and she is all bones.

ANGELA

[*Mildly.*]
I do not mind when she hits me. I am used to it.

CELLINI

But you must learn to mind it. You go through life as if you were a dream in a dream. Life may be a dream, but you are real. You must learn to believe that.

ANGELA

Sometimes I do not seem real to myself, but like someone I hear passing the house . . . late at night. You must think me very foolish.

CELLINI

I think you very beautiful.

ANGELA

I think you very handsome.

CELLINI

Why, I have never heard you so bold before!

ANGELA

I don't know. It just came out. . .

CELLINI

You must learn to say more things like it.

ANGELA

I will try.

CELLINI

And I will teach you. You are like flowing gold ready to be shaped into a woman.

ANGELA

I am not a child! I have known men.

CELLINI

[*Darkly.*]
I have heard: that foul mother of yours has sold you to villains. Well, she shall sell you to me, an honest man, by the grace of God!

ANGELA

She tells me that I must not like you, but I do anyway.

CELLINI

Turnips do not bear roses, nor carrion, swans! I

have it: Your mother is a gypsy and stole you from
the palace where you were born.

ANGELA

[*Smiling at the conceit.*]
I was born in a hut, by the river's edge.

CELLINI

Then the sea was your mother, and you came like
Venus, white and red on a sea blue wave, to the poor
earth-born.

ANGELA

You are making fun of me, again.

CELLINI

I am not making fun of you.

ANGELA

[*Alarmed.*]
Please stay where you are!

CELLINI

Listen to me, Angela, and try and understand
what my heart holds. To me you are the mystery
men must live on beyond bread; the wonder and the
glory of the world. Do you know that I am mad
about your hair? that I am furious about your
eyes? and that I am jealous that God, and not I,
created your body?

ANGELA

You must not come near me.

CELLINI

You are the matin in the morning, and the angelus in the evening; the bell which awakens me and the bell which says rest.

ANGELA

You must not come near me.

CELLINI

I love you like an angel, and I love you like a man, and I love you like a boy. I have had many women, but you are the first woman I have had, and I have not had you.

ANGELA

You must not come near me.

CELLINI

I must come very near you.

ANGELA

That is near enough.

CELLINI

[*Close to her.*]

I am miles away! It will take me years to reach you!

ANGELA

My mother has forbidden me——

CELLINI

What do I care what your mother forbids?

ANGELA

But I must do as she tells me!

CELLINI

You must think as I think and do as I do!
[BEATRICE, *chiefly distinguished from other
hags in appearance by a monstrous growth of
hair on her chin, has entered unobserved.
She plants herself between them suddenly.*]

BEATRICE

Oho!

CELLINI

[*In disgust.*]
Aha!

BEATRICE

[*Defiantly.*]
She must think as you think and do as you do, eh?

CELLINI

Yes, and not all the bawdy mothers in Italy shall
stop it.

BEATRICE

[*Grasping* ANGELA *roughly.*]

And that's the man you carry on with! [*To* CELLINI.] Assassin! I am an honest woman.

CELLINI

[*Controlling himself.*]
Honesty has a softer tone.

BEATRICE

[*Lost for words.*]
Everybody knows the kind of man you are.

CELLINI

Everybody knows I am the greatest man in Florence.

BEATRICE

Yah! You were suckled by a tiger.

CELLINI

[*Laying his hand on his dagger.*]
Beware, then, of my claw.

ANGELA

[*Beginning to weep.*]
Mother, come away from here.

BEATRICE

Away! at once!

CELLINI

You can't do that. It was agreed that Angela stay until my work was finished.

BEATRICE

It was not agreed that you set her against her own mother.

CELLINI

[*Losing his temper.*]
What sort of a mother are you?

BEATRICE

See! You do it before my very face.

CELLINI

Your face? That thing you wear cannot possibly be your face.

BEATRICE

O that my son were here to strike you down!

CELLINI

Your son? But he is busy seeking the name of his father.

BEATRICE

[*Intensely.*]
May you be blasted, inch by inch.

CELLINI

[*Shading his eyes as he looks at her.*]

I have noticed of late that you are growing a beard. You really shouldn't do it. It doesn't become you.

BEATRICE

[*Pushing* ANGELA *towards the exit left front.*]

Away! Away! [*To* CELLINI.] May your children be born in sties! [*She is hardly audible through her excitement.*] Away! Away!

CELLINI

[*Drawing his dagger.*]

If you step outside of that door I shall certainly kill you.

BEATRICE

[*As he approaches* ANGELA.]

Don't dare to touch her! If you touch her, I will swear to terrible things against you.

CELLINI

[*Taking* ANGELA *by the hand.*]

Swear away, old witch, and be sure your lies are good ones, for you will never tell any more.

BEATRICE

[*Croaking.*]

What do you want?

CELLINI

Angela.

BEATRICE

I had rather a worm was her bridegroom, than you!

CELLINI

Look out that a worm does not become your fifth husband, very soon, for I am sick and tired of your impudence. I love Angela with all my heart, and I will be good to her.

BEATRICE

And what about me?

CELLINI

You are to make yourself scarce.

BEATRICE

You ask me to give up my daughter?

CELLINI

You have no daughter. You have a property and I am willing to buy.

BEATRICE

[*Raising her glance on high.*]

Holy father! Did'st Thou make this man? who has no more respect for the feelings of a mother than to put things so plainly?

CELLINI

[*Impatiently.*]
Thirty ducats.

BEATRICE

[*Instantly.*]
Fifty ducats.

CELLINI

Too much.

BEATRICE

Not enough, you mean.

CELLINI

Thirty ducats.

BEATRICE

Fifty or nothing!

CELLINI

[*Turning to his work.*]
Nothing.

BEATRICE

Wait a minute: is fifty ducats too much for the shame my daughter brings on me by her wilful behavior?

CELLINI

Thirty ducats.

BEATRICE

Make it forty.

CELLINI

Done.

BEATRICE

And I am to see my daughter once a week.

CELLINI

[*At work again.*]
The deal is off.

BEATRICE

You haven't any consideration.

CELLINI

When you get the money, you leave the house, not to return. Is that agreed?

BEATRICE

[*Sighing.*]
You're hard on my feelings.

CELLINI

Yes, or no?

BEATRICE

I am a mother, and hate to lose my daughter, but when it's so plainly to her advantage, I'm not the one to stand in the way. Let it be as you say.

CELLINI

[*Jubilantly.*]
Heaven grants me my greatest desire.

BEATRICE

Not so fast. I haven't seen the color of your money, yet.

CELLINI

You shall see it directly. Gold never bought so much, before.

[*He kisses* ANGELA'S *hand, as* ASCANIO *dashes in.*]

ASCANIO

[*Breathlessly.*]
Master.

CELLINI

What the devil! My wedding day is my hanging day.

BEATRICE

[*Scenting difficulties.*]
But the agreement stands!

CELLINI

[*To* ASCANIO.]
What did the Cardinal say?

ASCANIO

That he would do what he could, but very much feared that you had gone too far, this time, for the Duke to listen to him.

BEATRICE

[*Aside to* ANGELO.]
What is this?

ANGELA

[*To* BEATRICE.]
He has killed two men.

CELLINI

[*To himself.*]
The Cardinal means that he will not put himself out for me. [*To* ASCANIO.] Go to the front of the house. Watch there. Let me know immediately if anyone comes. [ASCANIO *goes.*]

BEATRICE

You have killed two men? Then what about my money?

CELLINI

I said you should have it directly.

ANGELA

[*To* CELLINI.]
O Sir—Benvenuto—I pray that the Duke forgives you.

CELLINI

My fate is in the hands of my God, and there I trust it. In the meanwhile, I will not let myself be robbed at the very gate of heaven. [*To* BEA-

TRICE.]   Take Angela, and dress her in her loveli-
est gown.   Bring her to me and you shall have your
money.

BEATRICE
Good.   And if you are hanged afterwards——
[*As she reaches the exit.*]   So much the better!
[*They go.*]

CELLINI
[*Glaring after her.*]
What a Madonna she would make!   [*He turns,
and sees his forgotten work.*]   Judas accursed!   [*He
springs to the anvil and begins frantically beating
the gold.   There is a knocking at the rear door.*]

A VOICE
Open the door!

CELLINI
[*Advancing towards the door.*]
Who's there?
[ASCANIO *enters left.*]

ASCANIO
It's only Pier Landi, Master.

CELLINI
[*Calling through the door.*]
Pier, is anybody else about?

THE VOICE

No.   Open the door!

CELLINI

[*To* Ascanio *as he swings the bolt.*]
Idiot! Don't stand there! Get back to your post
and watch!
[Ascanio *exits.*]

PIER

[*As he enters.*]
One would think you feared the Holy Brother-
hood itself, with all your bolts and bars.

CELLINI

[*Locking the door.*]
I must be very careful, Pier, I am in great danger.
[Pier *smiles incredulously.*]   Pier, as I love you,
this is no joking matter.   Before the day is over,
I am likely to be nine feet tall.

PIER

In the name of the saints, what have you done,
now?

CELLINI

[*Brightening up.*]
Let me tell you all about it.   [*He takes his work
to the table and settles himself there as he has twice
before in relating his story.*]   I was coming through

the narrow street, when I noticed no less than six
fellows standing on one side, and more on the other.
I thought, Benvenuto, you had better look out!
Well, sure enough, as I came up to them, I saw
that one was Maffio! Taking the bull by the horns
and not waiting for them to attack me, I dashed
through the crowd, hitting and cutting until I had
laid two of the villains dead and wounded all of
the others. Maffio would have fled, but before he
could do so, I caught him and stabbed him so deeply
that I could not, for all of my strength, withdraw
the blade, but had to leave it sticking out of him
like a quill in a porcupine.

PIER
[*Pointing to* CELLINI's *sheath.*]
And that dagger?

CELLINI
[*Taken aback.*]
This— Another one!

PIER
[*Sardonically.*]
Now I would swear that is the dagger you always
carry!

CELLINI
[*Looking hard at him.*]
I said it was another.

PIER

It is the same.

CELLINI

[*In anger.*]
You doubt me?

PIER

No. I disbelieve you.

CELLINI

[*Hurt.*]
You presume on my affection.

PIER

Not at all. You see, I happened to witness the
fight.

CELLINI

[*Collapsing.*]
Then why did you let me make a fool of myself,
just now?

PIER

Because there is a quality to your lies which
should make you immortal. They are infinitely enjoyable, and make me realize again what a poor
thing truth is.

CELLINI

'You mock me, but I *did* kill Maffio.

PIER

I saw it, and it was bravely done. Only, there
were no others. He was alone. Besides, I know
you of old.

CELLINI

You are unjust to me. I am not a liar: I am
a poet. A liar is a man who makes much out of
nothing; but a poet is a man who makes more out
of a very little. I kill one man, and say that I
have killed three. And why not?

PIER

Why not, indeed?

CELLINI

Let me tell you, that in an age of saints, I should
be the greatest saint of all.

PIER

[*Smilingly.*]
St. Anthony, I suppose, should be jealous of your
temptations.

CELLINI

Yes. And St. Simon's perch, beside my own,
should look like a baby-chair by a throne! while the
maggots crawling over my body should make him
turn green with envy. But—this is no age of saints.

PIER

Amen.

CELLINI

This is an age of braggadocios; the wildest man rules. Well, seeing this is my youth, I set out to be the greatest braggadocio of them all: I make my deeds prodigious! legendary! Bourbon falls before my shot, and Italy rings with the fame of my terrible deeds!

PIER

So much so, that you are about to be hanged.

CELLINI

[*Proudly.*]
There are many who would rather be hanged as Cellini than live as themselves.

PIER

Still, I fancy that you had rather live as Cellini than be hanged as Cellini.

CELLINI

[*Making the sign of his faith.*]
God have me in his good keeping.

PIER

At the moment you are in the Duke's keeping, and I must warn you that he has forbidden the very mention of your name in his presence.

CELLIN'

[*Eagerly.*]
You have seen him?

PIER

[Gravely.]
That is why I am here.

CELLINI

Then tell me—quickly——

PIER

When I saw that Maffio was really dead, I hastened to his Excellency and pleaded your case. But he had already heard of the kiling, and, would not listen to me.

CELLINI

But what were his words?

PIER

[*Slowly.*]
He said: "Benvenuto thinks himself above the law. We must teach him that he is not. We have a lesson which will suffice forever."

CELLINI

[*Terror-stricken.*]
Those words are my death-warrant.

PIER

[*Strongly moved.*]
No, no, you despair too quickly.

CELLINI

You give me hope, but you do not believe it yourself. Oh, my dear Pier, do not give me hope! that branch that breaks over every precipice. But to die now, at the height of my manhood! when there is still marble in the earth! still gold in the furnace! To dangle in air where I have flown! and all because I rid the world of a scoundrel who killed my brother.

PIER

You must calm yourself. As I left the palace, I met the Cardinal and begged him to intercede.

CELLINI

The Cardinal is another villain.

PIER

Nevertheless, he told me that was his very mission.

CELLINI

The Cardinal will make a pretense of helping me, but he swims with the Duke's tide. Depend upon it. I am lost.
[EMILIA *appears at the door left.*]

CELLINI

[*Seeing her.*]
Well?

EMILIA

The signorina Beatrice says that Angela will soon be down and asks that you have the money ready.

CELLINI

[*To* PIER.]
I haven't told you the worst. [*To* EMILIA.] Tell Beatrice not to worry so much about the money and that I grow mighty impatient. [EMILIA *goes.*] For weeks, Pier, I have been haunted by a love for Angela, my model, and only this morning I found that she could be mine. [*Paces up and down excitedly.*] But I may still cheat these rabid fates. [ASCANIO, *white with fear, enters.*]

ASCANIO

Master! Forgive me! The Duke— I was talking to Emilia— The Duke is at the gate!
[CELLINI *gives him a box on the ears. A fanfare of trumpets sounds outside the rear door.*]

THE VOICE OF ANGELA

[*Calling from above.*]
Only a few minutes, Benvenuto!
[*Another fanfare sounds.*]

CELLINI

[*Despairingly.*]
Robbed before heaven!

A VOICE

[*Outside the door.*]
Open the door! In the name of the great Duke!

CELLINI

Stoned before Paradise!

THE VOICE OUTSIDE

Open the door! In the name of the Great Duke!
Open the door!

> [PIER, *with a gesture of helplessness, swings
> the bolt and door.* CELLINI *busies himself
> at the Anvil.* ASCANIO *looks on with wonder.
> Enter* ALESSANDRO, DUKE OF FLORENCE,
> *preceded and surrounded by his courtiers,
> including* OTTAVIANO *and* POLVERINO. *The
> DUKE is about* CELLINI'S *age. Among his
> own countrymen his swarthy skin has earned
> him the sobriquet of "The Moor." This base
> man, this bastard Medici who was no Medici,
> has features which are at once either sullen
> or childishly alive. At the moment, he is not
> up to the mark of his usual capacity for
> cruelty; he does not even relish the necessity
> of hanging* CELLINI. *The* DUKE, *in fact, is*

*in a mood for pleasure, and it is not unlikely
that he will gratify his mood to excess during
the next twenty-four hours. There is first
the annoyance of* CELLINI, *unfortunately.*]

THE DUKE

[*Scathingly.*]
Cellini.

CELLINI

My poor house is more than honored by the presence of Your Excellency.

THE DUKE

Your poor house would be more than honored by
the presence of any peaceful man.

POLVERINO

Capital, My Lord, capital!
[*Murmurs of applause from the others.*]

CELLINI

[*Looking at* POLVERINO.]
I fear that Your Excellency has been listening
to my enemies.

THE DUKE

Your crimes are your enemies.

CELLINI

My Lord, you are angry with me unjustly.

THE DUKE

[*To his courtiers.*]

Observe! he does not hesitate to rebuke even me. [*Murmurs against* CELLINI. *The* DUKE *addresses him.*] It is for us to judge the justice of our acts.

CELLINI

Your Excellency speaks truly, and for that very reason, your justice should lie beyond your anger, in the realms of your high intelligence.

POLVERINO

[*At the* DUKE'S *side*].

My Lord, will you listen longer to this outrageous fellow?

CELLINI

[*To* POLVERINO.]

Is it outrageous to believe that His Excellency has high intelligence?

POLVERINO

I won't bandy words with you.

CELLINI

Of course not: you lack the wit.

THE DUKE

[As POLVERINO *is about to reply.*]

Silence! We are here to put an end to argu-

ments, not to begin them. [*To* CELLINI.]   You
would teach me, then, my duty?

CELLINI

My Lord, you read offenses into my words which
are not there.

THE DUKE

Your offenses are everywhere.

CELLINI

On the tongues of my enemies.   But I protest
that I am a peaceful man.

POLVERINO

Your homicides are notorious.

CELLINI

[*Dangerously.*]
You would not dare to say that except in the
presence of My Lord!

THE DUKE

[To CELLINI.]
Am I to take that as proof of your peaceful
nature?

CELLINI

I try to pattern myself too much after Your
Excellency to be peaceful when I am insulted.

POLVERINO

My Lord——

THE DUKE

[*Pleased, to* POLVERINO.]
Come now, admit it was neatly said!

POLVERINO

Does my Lord forget this morning's murder?

THE DUKE

[*To* CELLINI, *frowning deeply.*]
Our lenience to you in the past has been greater
than that extended to any other of our subjects,
for we valued your service and gifts. You have
repaid our lenience by mocking it.

CELLINI

[*Fervently.*]
If that were true, no dungeon would be deep
enough to rot me, no tree high enough to swing
me.

THE DUKE

Only a short while ago, we pardoned a grave
crime, on condition that you keep the peace.

CELLINI

With all gratitude, I remember.

THE DUKE

In a strange, rough way, then. This morning,
in broad daylight, you spilled blood on the streets
of Florence, once again.

CELLINI

But in self-defense, my Lord.

THE DUKE

The time for leniency is past.

CELLINI

My Lord, all that I ask is, that having heard my
enemies, you hear me.

THE DUKE

We hear Maffio, also.

CELLINI

My Lord, he attacked me.

THE DUKE

We have heard differently.

CELLINI

[*Dramatically.*]
Attacked me, my Lord, with a whole regiment
of villains at his heels!

THE DUKE

[*To* Pier.]

You were there. Was there a regiment of them?

PIER

There was, my Lord.

THE DUKE

Come, now; on your honor?

PIER

[*Hesitant.*]

Well . . . perhaps not a regiment— [*More decisively.*] But enough of them.

POLVERINO

My Lord, he loves Cellini.

CELLINI

My Lord, are only those who hate me, to speak of me?

THE DUKE

Enough! I know my mind.

CELLINI

[*Throwing himself on his knees.*]

My Lord: I beseech you to give me leave to go
to France.

THE DUKE

The King of France is my friend, and I will not
wish you on him; within a week, his dominions would
be in an uproar. I might put you in prison; but
what's the use? When you are put in prison, you
break out! There is, however, a prison from which
there is no escape. Therefore, Cellini, in full justice, I sentence you to——

> [*As the* DUKE *is about to pronounce the
> fateful sentence, his eye catches* ANGELA, *as
> she appears in the door with* BEATRICE. *In
> a twinkling, his whole demeanor changes; his
> gravity falls away, his eye sparkles, and
> he forgets completely what he has been say-
> ing. The courtiers, astonished, turn to see
> what has distracted him, and exchange smiles
> among themselves.* CELLINI, *dazed, rises
> from his knees.*]

THE DUKE

[*With a smile to* CELLINI.]
This must be your masterpiece.

CELLINI

[*Glad at the respite.*]
She is my model, Your Excellency.

THE DUKE

The ancients never had such inspiration! [*To* ANGELA.] What is your name, my child?

ANGELA

Angela, my Lord.

THE DUKE

[*To* CELLINI.]
Has she a lover, Benvenuto?

CELLINI

[*Confused.*]
No, My Lord.

THE COURTIERS

[*Among themselves.*]
Did you hear? He called him Benvenuto! On my word he did! [*Etc.*]

THE DUKE

[*To* ANGELA.]
Come over to me, my child.

BEATRICE

[*Pushing* ANGELA.]
Quick! Quick! Over to him! he said.
[ANGELA *comes down, center stage, while* BEATRICE, *jumping with excitement, remains by the door.*]

THE DUKE

Do you like me, Angela?

ANGELA

Yes, My Lord.

THE DUKE

[*Delighted.*]

"My Lord!"   [*To his gentlemen.*]   Would that all my subjects looked like her!   [*To* ANGELA.]   Has anyone ever told you that you were adorable?

ANGELA

Yes, My Lord.

THE DUKE

[*Playfully.*]

But you haven't listened to them?

ANGELA

[*Not knowing what to say.*]

Yes, My Lord.

BEATRICE

[*From the door.*]

She means, no, My Lord!

THE DUKE

[*To* BEATRICE.]

Who are you?

BEATRICE

Her mother, Your Excellency.

THE DUKE

[*Glancing from one to the other.*]
Nonsense! There must be some mistake! [*To* ANGELA.] Is she really your mother?

ANGELA

Yes, My Lord.

THE DUKE

How peculiar! She looks like a goat—doesn't she?

BEATRICE

If you say so, My Lord.

THE DUKE

[*To* ANGELA.]
While you. . . [*Overcome in his admiration.*] Well, you certainly don't look like a goat. I have taken quite a fancy to you. [POLVERINO *whispers in the* DUKE'S *ear. The* DUKE *answers him with pleasure.*] By all means! By all means! [POLVERINO *crosses to* BEATRICE. *The* DUKE *to* ANGELA.] How would you like me to take you away from here?

POLVERINO

[*Slipping a purse to* BEATRICE *while* ANGELA *struggles for a reply to the* DUKE.]

His Excellency desires to show your daughter the
Summer Palace.

ANGELA
[*To the* DUKE, *finally.*]
I am very happy here, My Lord.

BEATRICE
[*To* POLVERINO.]
That this honor should come to me!

THE DUKE
[*"The thing is settled."*]
You will be happier with me.

CELLINI
[*In an agony of emotion.*]
Your Excellency——

THE DUKE
[*To* CELLINI, *forcing a serious expression.*]
Silence! I am considering your case.
   [*He smiles gayly at* ANGELA *and strokes her
    hair.*]

BEATRICE
[*To* POLVERINO.]
I'll run upstairs and throw a few things together.
   [*As she goes,* EMILIA *enters and stands in
    wide-eyed awe at the gathering.*]

THE DUKE

[*To* ANGELA.]
You will like the Summer Palace.

ANGELA

My Lord, I am very happy here.

THE DUKE

Do not say that again. You will displease me.

CELLINI

[*In a sweat.*]
But, My Lord, it is impossible!

THE DUKE

[*Not believing his ears.*]
What do you say?

CELLINI

She is my model. I must have her for my work.

THE DUKE

[*Deciding to be good-humored.*]
Then get another model!

CELLINI

But I have half-finished a statue for which she is
posing!

THE DUKE

[*To* ANGELA.]

Does Cellini cross you in everything, as he does
me?

ANGELA

He has been good to me.

CELLINI

Your Excellency——

OTTAVIANO

[*Emerging from the crowd, aside to* CELLINI.]

Be still, you fool! Don't you see that the girl has
saved you?

CELLINI

[*Brushing him aside.*]

My Lord, the girl is attached to me.

THE DUKE

I am glad to hear it. Since she has an affectionate
nature, she will become attached to me.

ANGELA

My Lord, I do not desire to go.

THE DUKE

You do not desire to go?

ANGELA

I am happy here, I have friends.

THE DUKE

Is that all? Well, then, we shall take your friends with us. [*He spies* EMILIA.] Is that one of your friends? [ANGELA *inclines her head.*]

THE DUKE

[*To* EMILIA.]
Come here, my child. [EMILIA, *transfixed, nevertheless manages to reach the* DUKE.] What is your name, little one?

EMILIA

Emilia, My Lord.

THE DUKE

Emilia, you are to come to the Summer Palace with Angela. Do you understand?

EMILIA

Yes, My Lord.

THE DUKE
[*To* ANGELA *as* EMILIA *clasps her.*]
There: now you have your friend and you will not be lonely.

ANGELA

[*Obstinately.*]
I am very happy here, My Lord.
[BEATRICE *enters and hears* ANGELA.]

THE DUKE

[*Perplexed.*]

But what is there here that you will not have at the Palace?

BEATRICE

Nothing, My Lord, nothing! The girl doesn't know her own good.

THE DUKE

[*To* ANGELA.]

Aha! It is your mother that you want. Well, she shall come along, too. [*To* BEATRICE.] To your daughter, goat-face! [BEATRICE *goes to* ANGELA *and surreptitiously pinches her. The* DUKE *rubs his hands with satisfaction.*] And now, everything is arranged. Let us go.

POLVERINO

My Lord, you forget Maffio.

THE DUKE

The deuce! Of course, I never can remember anything. [*To* CELLINI.] Have you finished that medal for me?

CELLINI

It is under way, My Lord.

THE DUKE

Well, I can't hang you until it is finished, that's certain. Ottaviano, where's Ottaviano?

OTTAVIANO

[*Stepping forward.*]
Here, Alessandro.

THE DUKE

I have delayed too long. Stay behind and show
the design you have made for the medal's reverse.

OTTAVIANO

It is an interesting design, Cousin.

THE DUKE

Really? Walk a few steps and tell me about it.
I want to be sure that the design is worthy of me.
Cellini will await your return. Ready?

POLVERINO

My Lord, you still forget—Cellini.

THE DUKE

Of course—again. Just like me. Cellini! It is
our command that you do not leave Florence—
[*With a glance at* ANGELA.] No, that you do not
leave this house, until our final judgment is rendered.

CELLINI

You are very good, My Lord.

THE DUKE

Not at all. I shall probably hang you yet. You deserve it. And now, forward. [*Exit the soldiers, then* BEATRICE, EMILIA *and* ANGELA.] Gentlemen——

PIER

[*Aside to* CELLINI.]
I go with the Duke to do what I can.

THE DUKE

Gentlemen: About this little matter of Angela. . . . It will not be necessary to mention it to the Duchess.

> [*The Courtiers signify that they understand. The* DUKE *passes out.* OTTAVIANO, POLVERINO, PIER *and* COURTIERS *follow.* CELLINI *is left in the foreground;* ASCANIO *runs up the steps and watches his disappearing love.*]

ASCANIO

Emilia!

CELLINI

[*Wildly, as the last courtier exits.*]
Angela! O! that I had my hands on Polverino's throat!

> [*He gives an inarticulate cry, and overcome by his feelings, goes.* ASCANIO, *after a doubtful moment, makes a grave decision and bolts,*

right rear. But in a moment his voice is heard protestingly.]

ASCANIO'S VOICE

Let me pass.

A VOICE

[*Sternly.*]
Back, I said, back you go!
[Ascanio, *prodded by the sword of a* SOLDIER, *is forced into the room.*]

ASCANIO

[*Between pleading and objecting.*]
You have no right—the Duke's orders are to hold my master here, not me.
[*He draws a small dagger.*]

THE SOLDIER

[*Roughly, advancing with his sword.*]
Put down that pin!
[Ascanio, *in fright, drops behind the work-bench. The* SOLDIER *exiting, salutes* OTTAVIANO, *as the latter returns.*]

OTTAVIANO

[*Displeased at his reception.*]
Cellini! Where are you, Cellini?
[CELLINI *comes in bearing an urn.*]

CELLINI

Sir, you must pardon my absence, but I desired to be alone for a while.

OTTAVIANO

When we desire to be alone, we are generally sorrowful.

CELLINI

[*Smolderingly.*]
Sorrowful? No, sir, I was dreaming that I had my hands on Polverino's throat.

OTTAVIANO

Polverino? The Duke's procurer. A foul fellow, a stinking fellow.

CELLINI

[*Breaking loose.*]
Do I not procure beauty for His Excellency? Do I not pander loveliness to him? Yes—but no more!
[*He smashes the urn on the floor.*]

OTTAVIANO

Cellini, I want to tell you what I have in mind for the Duke's reverse.

CELLINI

[*Studying him.*]
The medal's reverse, sir.

OTTAVIANO

Of course.   By the way, can we be heard from the house?

CELLINI

The walls of this house are strong enough to keep out the noise of this shop.

OTTAVIANO

Good.   Then let me tell you that I have high hopes of fulfilling the Duke's command: to create a design worthy of him.
[*He draws his hand across his throat in sinister fashion.*]

CELLINI

[*Starting.*]
Sir, there is danger in that design.

OTTAVIANO

Not necessarily.   Let me tell you more about this.

CELLINI

I shall be delighted to hear.

OTTAVIANO

Cellini, I just thought of a curious thing which happened last week in the city. A man was found dead, with a great gash in his head. Perhaps you heard of it?

CELLINI

Pier mentioned something of the matter.

OTTAVIANO

I knew the man, slightly; a charming fellow, with an innumerable number of indecent stories; but during my too-brief acquaintance with him, I discovered that he had one grave fault; he was indiscreet. On my word—indiscreet.

CELLINI

He told things?

OTTAVIANO

Oh, they were harmless enough things . . . but still, don't you think that he was a very silly fellow?

CELLINI

An absurd fellow, sir.

OTTAVIANO

I knew that you should agree with me. Now, about this design, for the medal. It is in the form of a knife.

CELLINI

A sharp idea——

OTTAVIANO

Hilt up——

CELLINI

For heaven——

OTTAVIANO

Point down——

CELLINI

For hell——

OTTAVIANO

And a strong arm behind it!

CELLINI

A masterful conception! A noble conception! But with all my skill at my craft, I do not see how the design can be carried out.

OTTAVIANO

The process is a simple one. I furnish the outline and you furnish . . . the metal.

CELLINI

And then?

OTTAVIANO

Why, when the thing is ready, you strike.

CELLINI

Where?

OTTAVIANO

[*Laying his hand on his heart.*]
Here.

CELLINI

[*Admiringly.*]
Sir, you are a subtle man.

OTTAVIANO

[*Deprecatingly.*]
Quite plain-spoken, I assure you.

CELLINI

You are too modest.

OTTAVIANO

By no means. There are matters, after all, which
require us to be subtle before we can express them
intelligently. Otherwise, they might appear crude,
and perhaps even improper! Indeed, it is not too
much to say, about such matters, that when one is
most subtle, one is most plain-spoken. Thus, a common man, with a certain thought in his head, might
say— [*In a sudden, terrible voice.*] My brother
must die!

CELLINI

Sir, I had a brother once. I loved him with all
my soul.

OTTAVIANO

And it does you credit. I, too, love my brother;
I would not harm a hair on his head! Therefore,
wishing him long life, I say— [*In the same terrible
voice.*] The *Duke* must die!

CELLINI

And you find a difference in the words?

OTTAVIANO

A profound difference: for the Duke dies, but my
brother lives on . . . in my heart.

CELLINI

He cannot wine, dine, or embrace his loves there!

OTTAVIANO

So long as I do all those things, he does them
with me. For the little of life that he loses, we
give him eternity; while the violence of his end as-
sures him of forgiveness for his sins, which otherwise
might damn him.

CELLINI

In short, we do him a favor.

OTTAVIANO

A lasting favor. And there you see, that what
in a common light might appear a cruel business,
is in reality a generous act.

CELLINI

Sir, I am only a poor sculptor, and must fear
the consequences of a generous act which is also an
act of treason.

OTTAVIANO

Your fears are unnecessary. Treason is the re-
bellion of a subject against the justly powerful:
When one of the powerful himself undertakes to
rule, it is not treason, but an act of virtue.

CELLINI

A virtue?   Of what nature?

OTTAVIANO

Of the nature of courage: because he exercises
boldly one of the attributes of his royalty; to domi-
nate. Here again, you see that what in a common
light might appear to be an act of treason, is in
reality in thorough accord with the laws of society.
And how fortunately! Since the death of the duke
is to my advantage, and even more to your own.

CELLINI

I think it is more to your advantage, Sir, than
to mine.

OTTAVIANO

On the contrary, for if the Duke lives, I live, but
you will certainly die.

CELLINI

And if you succeed, I die.

OTTAVIANO

Give me one good reason!

CELLINI

You will not need a good reason.

OTTAVIANO

Hang the man who helped me gain power?

CELLINI

That will be your reason.

OTTAVIANO

A strange one!

CELLINI

Then, again, you will see my execution is not—
as might appear in a common light—an act of
treachery, but an act of justice, since in murdering
the Duke, I disobeyed your wishes, and murdered
your brother as well.

OTTAVIANO

I should keep you with me as one of the stars of
my reign.

CELLINI

One of the stars that droop in the morning sky.

OTTAVIANO

Cellini, you have changed your tone!

CELLINI

I protest, Sir, I have not.

OTTAVIANO

[*In a cold rage.*]

Cellini, you have played with me. You must proceed with the design.

CELLINI

I am always ready to proceed with the design, for the Duke's medal.

OTTAVIANO

If the Duke lives, you shall be hanged twice; once by him, and once by me.

CELLINI

If I am under the Duke's arrest, I am also under his protection, Sir.

OTTAVIANO

The Duke is an ass. And you are a fool!

CELLINI

Sir, I have been remembering who you are. But you impugn my honor.

OTTAVIANO

[*Sincerely.*]

Fellows like yourself are not called upon to have honor. That rests with me and my sort.

CELLINI

Sir, Florence was named after one of my family.

OTTAVIANO

[*Staggering back.*]
What! No thunder? No lightning? Still there?
Then there is no God!

CELLINI

My house is honored by your presence, Sir, but
my dinner waits.

OTTAVIANO

And so must your appetite. For I must tell you,
that when you are hanged, and the Duke is tired of
Angela, I shall enjoy her.

CELLINI

[*Half-drawing his blade.*]
This is unbearable.

OTTAVIANO

It is death to touch that in the presence of a
Medici. Come now, be sensible. [*As he turns to go,*
CELLINI *again half-pulls his dagger.*] Think it over!
I shall drop back in an hour or so. Cellini, there
was a man found dead in the city, last week, with
a great gash in his head. There was no inquiry.
[OTTAVIANO *pushes* CELLINI's *dagger back in place.*

He walks to the rear door and looks out on the scene, which has darkened a little.] Ah! The sun and moon are both in the sky: It will be a beautiful evening. Cellini, come here! [CELLINI, *after hesitating, crosses to him.* ASCANIO *takes advantage of the clear foreground to dart out.*] Look out there, my friend; don't you feel how good a thing it is to be alive? To see that moon rising like a silver ghost from the burning grave of the sun? Think of it—not to see the evening or the morning! Not to hunt the spirit lost in nature—not to touch warm flesh—but to be wrapped forever in a hideous futility! We're wise to hold on to things as long as we can! And yet, there are fools who throw all this away out of sheer pig-headedness! I can't abide them. Well, a good appetite and expect me later. [*He goes, with a gracious wave of his hand.*]

CELLINI

[*To himself.*]
Swine!

ASCANIO

[*Running in from left breathlessly.*]
Master—The Duchess is here—she's coming through the house——

CELLINI

[*Closing the rear door.*]
The Duchess!

[*Enter the* DUCHESS *of Florence, and several
of her ladies. The* DUCHESS *is not good-
looking, in any conventional sense; but she is
an imperious, charming woman. . . . As-
CANIO exits. The* DUCHESS *acknowledges*
CELLINI'S *obeisance with a frown.*]

THE DUCHESS

[*Left center.*]
I hear that you have been disgracing yourself
again, Cellini.

CELLINI

[*Right center.*]
If I am in disgrace with My Lady, then I must
have done something wrong. But I cannot imagine
what it can be.

THE DUCHESS

Cannot imagine! A firebrand fighting in the
streets with a knife like any other ruffian. Fine play
for a man of your talents!

CELLINI

I thank Your Ladyship.

THE DUCHESS

Has that husband of mine been here?

CELLINI

He has, My Lady.

THE DUCHESS

When are you to be hanged?

CELLINI

Unfortunately I don't know, My Lady. His Excellency has forbidden me to leave the house until final judgment is rendered. It is very hard on me.

THE DUCHESS

I am surprised. The Duke left me with the intention of hanging you. [*Suspiciously.*] There must have been a woman around. Was there?

CELLINI

[*Lying nobly.*]
No, My Lady.

THE DUCHESS

It is generally a woman that distracts him. But it does not become me to talk to such a badly-behaved specimen as yourself.

CELLINI

I am sorry at your anger, My Lady.

THE DUCHESS

You may be, for I have no use for you—none at
all. I came here to show these ladies that exquisite
salt-cellar which you have been making for me.
Where is it?

CELLINI

In the other workshop, downstairs, Madam. I
will have it brought here at once.

THE DUCHESS

Nothing of the sort. Let the ladies see it in its
native setting. Who will show it to them?

CELLINI

My apprentice, Your Excellency. Ascanio! [*The
latter appears.*] Show these ladies the salt-cellar.
[Ascanio *exits with them.*]

THE DUCHESS

[*Dropping her severe air as abruptly as did
the* Duke *when he saw* Angela.]
And now, my dear Benvenuto, I can forget that
I am the Duchess.

CELLINI

My Lady overpowers me.

THE DUCHESS

I can remember that I am a woman.

CELLINI

[*Gallantly.*]
It is one of Your Ladyship's glories.

THE DUCHESS

You were pleased by my calling you . . . Benvenuto?

CELLINI

Infinitely pleased.

THE DUCHESS

One would not think that I afforded you infinite pleasure from your actions towards me.

CELLINI

[*Nervously gallant.*]
I never make a beautiful thing without thinking of My Lady.

THE DUCHESS

Benvenuto, have you ever noticed that when you are near me, I do not always treat you as if I were the Duchess?

CELLINI

[*Resolved to be obtuse.*]
No, My Lady.

THE DUCHESS

Then you are a nincompoop.

CELLINI

My father was also of that opinion.   He desired
me to study the accursed flute——

THE DUCHESS

Drat your father!   I am interested in you.

CELLINI

Your Ladyship is good to me beyond my wildest
dreams.

THE DUCHESS

I was annoyed with you, today.   You sent to the
Cardinal and begged him to intercede for you.

CELLINI

A drowning man will clutch at a straw.

THE DUCHESS

There are firmer reeds for you to lean on.   Why
did you not send to me?

CELLINI

I dared not hope so high.

THE DUCHESS

Then you are not the man I took you for, Benvenuto. You have a good friend in me.

CELLINI

Had I only known!

THE DUCHESS

You might have a better friend, in me.

CELLINI

What shall I do, My Lady?

THE DUCHESS

Stop pretending to be a fool.

CELLINI

[*After a pause.*]
I dare not, My Lady.

THE DUCHESS

Benvenuto, are you afraid?

CELLINI

Not at all, My Lady. Life is not easy: if we are lucky, we are offered, and perhaps only once, gifts so precious that not to take them seems blasphemous. Our blood leaps up, and our hands, our hearts, reach out . . . and there we must stop.

THE DUCHESS

And pray, why, if not in fear?

CELLINI

Because of that little part of our soul which we call, "honor."

THE DUCHESS

[*Indignantly.*]

Honor, indeed! Your masculine metaphysics are enough to turn an honest woman's stomach. Honor! that shining name which men use to cover their cowardice. Faugh! I am disappointed in you.

CELLINI

What can I say that will atone?

THE DUCHESS

Nothing. Your first love was a chisel and your last will be a hammer.

CELLINI

My Lady, you wrong me. I am capable of great love.

THE DUCHESS

You? Never! It is the tragedy of great ladies to discover that great men make poor lovers. They do not love women; they use them. That is why we generally marry half-wits.

CELLINI

It is a very tempting challenge that you make, My Lady.

THE DUCHESS

I meant to take you with me to the Summer Palace, to devise a decoration for the fountain.

CELLINI

[*Starting.*]
The Summer Palace!

THE DUCHESS

Yes, the Duke asked me to go, this morning, and I said I would not. But I have changed my mind; I shall be there tonight.

CELLINI

That will be a joyful surprise for him, I'm sure.

THE DUCHESS

He was happy when I said no. What do you say? Will you come down . . . to look at the fountain?

CELLINI

The Duke has bound me to my house.

THE DUCHESS

I will protect you.

CELLINI

My Lady, I will risk all to get to the Summer Palace!— [*As an afterthought.*] For you. [*He kisses her hand.*]

THE DUCHESS

Spoken like a man! [*She takes a key out of her bosom.*] You know the balcony?— My door?

CELLINI

I have gazed up at it a thousand times in desolation.

THE DUCHESS

We shall console you for that, tonight.

[*She hands him the key. Then, as he kisses her hand, and is about to kiss her on the lips,* THE LADIES *reënter.*]

FIRST LADY

[*To the* DUCHESS.]

Madam, that little thing will be the wonder of the ages.

SECOND LADY

[*To* CELLINI.]
It would grace the table of Lucullus.

THE DUCHESS

[*Severely.*]
Do not spoil him with your compliments; he does not deserve them; he is a wicked man. I have just been giving him a piece of my mind. Cellini, I go; mind what I have said.

CELLINI

To the last syllable, My Lady.
> [*He bows them out, right rear. Taking the key from his pocket, he looks at it—smilingly.*]

ACT II

It is quite dark, as the curtain rises, and a song is heard. The scene imperceptibly lightens until we see an exquisite spot in a garden, flanked in the center and left-rear by a high stone wall, while adjoining this, left, is a gate which leads into other portions of the garden of the Summer Palace. A path runs, left and right, and leads, right, to the Palace. It is ANGELA *who is singing the song which we have heard, and she is seated with* EMILIA *on a bench to the left-front of the wall. The moonlight falls profusely on the bench; elsewhere, the greenery lies in shadow except for stray beams.* ANGELA *finishes her song and both girls sigh deeply.*

EMILIA

[*At last.*]
You shouldn't have sung. They might have heard.

ANGELA

I couldn't helping singing. I felt so sad. I don't know why.

EMILIA

It was a lovely song. It made me think about things . . . that I couldn't think about.

ANGELA

When I sing, I feel as if something were healing in me, while my heart is breaking.

EMILIA

Don't you think we'd better go back? We must, soon, or they'll be looking for us.

ANGELA

Not yet. Let us sit a while and dream . . . of things that aren't.

EMILIA

When you talk that way, you make me think of Ascanio. I don't want to think of him.

ANGELA

[*Smiling faintly.*]
Not at all?

EMILIA

. . . . I really want to think of him all the time.

ANGELA

And I remember the Master—Benvenuto.

EMILIA

[*Sharply.*]
You mustn't remember him. He is a bad man. He kills people right and left.

ANGELA

He was good to me.

EMILIA

Because he wanted you.

ANGELA

I know.   And sometimes, I would like . . .

EMILIA

You haven't gone and fallen in love with him?

ANGELA

[*Shaking her head.*]
I am not in love with him.   I am not in love with
anybody.   I wish that I were.   I should like to know
what it means to love.

EMILIA

[*Scandalized.*]
Haven't you ever been in love?

ANGELA

Never.   When men come to me, like the Master,
with such a strange look in their eyes, I wonder at
them.

EMILIA

I have been in love, often.

ANGELA

How often?

EMILIA

Let me see. There was . . . of course! And there was—but he doesn't count, he only lasted a day. And . . . yes. . . . Well, four times before Ascanio. With him, ten, because he counts twice as much as all the others.

ANGELA

[*Rather wistfully.*]
And how does it feel, to fall in love?

EMILIA

Sometimes, as if you were lying on those clouds, up there in the skies.

ANGELA

That must be delightful.

EMILIA

Sometimes, as if you had picked up a purse in the street and found it full of ducats.

ANGELA

That must be joyful.

EMILIA

But sometimes, as if you had hit your thumb—hard—with a hammer.

ANGELA

That must be painful.

EMILIA

Oh, it is! You swear never to fall in love again.
But then—the thumb heals, and before you know it,
bang! You have hit it with another hammer.

ANGELA

That's silly.

EMILIA

It seems so, but it isn't. . . When you were
singing, I dreamed that I was up there, on those
clouds. Ascanio was behind me, on another cloud,
and he was trying to catch me, but I kept a little
ahead of him, all the while.

ANGELA

I have never been in love, but I understand that.
I like men to chase me.

EMILIA

. . . Then he began calling me names, but I
only laughed at him. So he changed his tune, and
begged me to stop. I did stop, but just when he
could have stepped onto my cloud—I pushed it away,
and was off again!

ANGELA

I understand that, too, although it was cruel.

EMILIA

I don't know why it is, but it is pleasant to be cruel to the man you love.

ANGELA

To all men.

EMILIA

But in the end, you see, you are not cruel. You take his face between your hands and kiss him on the mouth—long . . . And, then you run away again.

ANGELA

That is cruel, too.

EMILIA

Yes, but he is glad to be miserable, because he has the joy of catching you again.

ANGELA

But some of them run away from you.

EMILIA

Sure, all of them do. But I go after them.

ANGELA

Far?

EMILIA

To the end of the world.

ANGELA

I have made men love me. . . Would you throw your arms around a man who didn't want you?

EMILIA

Certainly . . . for then he would want me.

ANGELA

I've tried to fall in love with all the men I have known . . . with the Master . . . with the Duke. And if they are good-looking, they are all the same to me.

EMILIA

I think your mother has put the Evil Eye on you.

ANGELA

Perhaps that is it! She leaned over me in my cradle and put the Evil Eye on me. [*They cross themselves.*] I have wished . . . sometimes, that my mother was dead.

EMILIA

You'd be better off.

ANGELA

Do you think it wicked?

EMILIA

Yes, but I'd wish it, too, if I were you.

ANGELA

Perhaps if she were dead, I should learn to love.

EMILIA

That might kill the Evil Eye.

ANGELA

I will pray that she dies.

EMILIA

[*Scared.*]
No, not now!

ANGELA

O Lord! if my mother must die before I can begin
to love . . . do not let her live.

EMILIA

I wish you had waited . . . when I wasn't around.
. . . [*With a little scream.*]   Sh-sh!   Someone's
coming.

ANGELA

Where?

EMILIA

[*Pointing, right.*]
Don't you see?

ANGELA

Men.

EMILIA

Let's run.

ANGELA

It's too late. We're seen.

EMILIA

[*Clutching her.*]
And they're soldiers!

POLVERINO'S VOICE

[*Off, right.*]
My Lord, I'm sure it's Angela.
[*Enter the* DUKE *and Gentlemen, including*
POLVERINO.]

THE DUKE

Is that you, Angela?

ANGELA

It is, My Lord.

THE DUKE

What a start you have given me! We thought
you had fled.

ANGELA

My Lord, it was stuffy inside; we came out for the
air.

THE DUKE

You came out late, then. Your mother thought
that Cellini had kidnaped you, and I swore to hang
him in the morning. Polverino, remind me not to

hang him; otherwise I shall forget. Let me see—
there was something else I had to say; what was it?

POLVERINO

My Lord——
  [*Whispers in his ear.*]

THE DUKE

That was it. [*Admiringly.*] I do wish that I had
a memory like yours, Polverino: I should hang more
people than I do. [*To* ANGELA.] He has told me.
So great was your mother's excitement, when you
could not be found, that she had a stroke.

EMILIA

Oh!——

ANGELA

  [*Stunned.*]
She is not dead?

THE DUKE

  [*Uninterested.*]
Not yet, I believe.

ANGELA

You mean . . . she will die?

THE DUKE
  [*Shrugging his shoulder.*]

Not likely. She looks like a goat and will probably climb the rocks of her sickness as if she were one. In fact, I think that she is one.

ANGELA

I must go to her.

THE DUKE

You must stay here, with me. There is nothing that you can do for her; she is well taken care of. Polverino will bring us word if there is any change.

POLVERINO

On the instant, My Lord.

THE DUKE

Gentlemen.
   [*They are dismissed, and go.*]

ANGELA

   [*Pausing.*]
My Lord . . . when was my mother stricken?

THE DUKE

Just before we found you. We had been racking the palace for your fair forms. When you were nowhere to be seen, the old lady gave a cry and dropped down as though struck by a bolt from heaven.

EMILIA

[*Breaking into a mounting wail.*]
Oh, Angela! Did you hear what he said?

THE DUKE

[*Astonished.*]
What's wrong with it? I thought it rather eloquent, myself. [*To* ANGELA.] One would think it were her mother, and not yours, the way you both behave.

ANGELA

[*Quickly.*]
It is not that, My Lord. Your presence frightens her.

THE DUKE

[*Pleased.*]
Does it, now? Really? [*Patting* EMILIA.] There's no necessity to carry on so. Even if I am the Duke, I'm not a bad fellow.

ANGELA

My Lord, you frightened me, also, this morning.

THE DUKE

[*More than pleased.*]
Did I, now? Really? But you have learned not to be afraid of me?

ANGELA

Yes, My Lord.

THE DUKE

You know, I'm particularly glad that you take this matter of your mother so sensibly. [*With wholly unconscious egoism.*] I was rather afraid it had spoiled my evening.

ANGELA

My Lord, I do not love my mother overmuch.

THE DUKE

Don't you, now? That's splendid. I don't like her myself. I never trust a woman who has whiskers.

ANGELA

She has not been very good to me, My Lord.

THE DUKE

Hasn't she? Then, that's probably why she was struck down. [EMILIA *gives vent to a new outburst of horror. The* DUKE *is thoroughly annoyed.*] Stop that! [*To* ANGELA.] Does she always go on like this? Because, I won't have it! I once had a mistress— [*Pausing with unexpected delicacy; then, to* ANGELA.] You don't mind?

ANGELA

It is quite all right, My Lord.

THE DUKE

Thank you. Some women dislike so much hearing about the other women. . . I was saying, that I once had a mistress who would cry at the slightest provocation . . . when her husband died, for instance, or when a new dress was late in delivery, or at any other time. Whenever you went to see her you were certain to come home wet to the skin. I finally married her again to a fellow I disliked. But . . . where were we?

ANGELA

My Lord, we were talking of my mother.

THE DUKE

An ugly subject: let us drop it. Let me see. . . [*An inspiration.*]   Emilia, go back to the palace.

ANGELA

My Lord, I should rather that she stayed with me.

THE DUKE

Don't vex me.   [*To* EMILIA.]   If you don't want to go into the palace, you can stay in the gardens. But don't bother us. And don't peek.   [EMILIA *exits, rear.*]   Thank goodness, we're alone!

ANGELA

[*Softly.*]
My Lord, you desired to be alone with me.

THE DUKE

[*Fervently.*]
Forever.

ANGELA

Forever?

THE DUKE

Well . . . until tomorrow, at least.　And you
. . . are you glad to be alone with me?

ANGELA

My Lord, I am glad.

THE DUKE

[*Kissing her hand.*]
Angela, when we are alone, don't call me "My
Lord."　I prefer that you call me—Bumpy.　It's my
nickname.

ANGELA

I scarcely dare, My Lord.

THE DUKE

It is my wish.　But only in private, mind you—
never in public; it would dethrone me.　Now, let me
hear you say it—Bumpy! like that.

ANGELA

Bumpy. . .

THE DUKE

Splendid!　You got it without any trouble, didn't

you? Some of them have a devil of a time with it!—
I beg your pardon. There I go again. I shouldn't
have said that.

ANGELA

It is quite all right, My Lord.

THE DUKE

[*Correcting her.*]
Bumpy.

ANGELA

Bumpy.

THE DUKE

Tell me, when you saw me this morning, were you
taken with me?

ANGELA

Yes, Bumpy.

THE DUKE

Could you love me?

ANGELA

I want to learn to love you, very much.

THE DUKE

And by St. Costanzo, you shall!

ANGELA

I want to long for you . . . when you are away.

THE DUKE

[*Vastly flattered.*]
You want me as much as all that?

ANGELA

I want to want you . . . as much as all that.

THE DUKE

Let us begin to make you want me. First, you
don't dislike my face?

ANGELA

No, My Lord.

THE DUKE

[*Correcting her.*]
Bumpy.

ANGELA

[*Obediently.*]
Bumpy.

THE DUKE

[*Resuming.*]
You don't dislike my face. Well, that's half the
battle. You find some of my features even pleasing,
perhaps.

ANGELA

I do, Bumpy.

THE DUKE

My . . . forehead, let us say?

ANGELA

Yes, Bumpy.

THE DUKE

[*Leaning still closer.*]
My . . . eyes?

ANGELA

Yes, Bumpy.

THE DUKE

[*Leaning closer to her.*]
My . . . nose?

ANGELA

[*Hesitantly.*]
Yes.

THE DUKE

Oh! You're not so sure about my nose! . . . My
mouth?

> [*She does not reply, for he kisses her las-*
> *civiously.* POLVERINO *enters and stands*
> *aghast at the scene he must interrupt.*]

POLVERINO

[*In a small voice.*]
My Lord! [*No answer. He raises his voice.*]
My Lord! My Lord!

THE DUKE

[*Hears, flares at him.*]
Polverino! How dare you!

ANGELA

[*Springing to her feet.*]
My mother is dead.

POLVERINO

Worse! The Duchess has arrived.

THE DUKE

[*Stupidly.*]
The Duchess?

POLVERINO

Yes, My Lord.

THE DUKE

[*Lacking confirmation.*]
My wife?

POLVERINO

[*Specifically.*]
Your wife, the Duchess, My Lord.

THE DUKE

Here?

POLVERINO

Not three minutes ago.

THE DUKE
[*A gross betrayal of faith.*]
But she told me that she would stay in town.

POLVERINO
Her Excellency desires me to acquaint you with
the fact that she changed her mind, and awaits you.

THE DUKE
Is it a trap?

POLVERINO
A trap, My Lord?

THE DUKE
Does she know that Angela is here?

POLVERINO
No, My Lord.
THE DUKE
Why do you say that?

POLVERINO
Her Excellency is quiet and composed.

THE DUKE
A bad sign. You don't know that woman, Polverino! When she merely taps her foot, the walls
of Jericho are falling. [*Looks at* ANGELA.] The

Duchess is so unreasonable about these matters,
Polverino. What must we do?

POLVERINO

Tell the Duchess that one of the gentlemen
brought the girl here.

THE DUKE

I said you did not know her; she would guess that
I was the gentleman. We must think of something
else.

POLVERINO

My Lord, we can send the girl away.

THE DUKE

[*Disgusted.*]
I could think of that myself.

POLVERINO

[*Pausing.*]
My Lord, the Duchess said that she was weary
from the journey and would retire early.

THE DUKE

Immediately, I hope. Well?

POLVERINO

Let the girl stay here, My Lord, until you have

seen Her Excellency. Then, you can return, and we
can devise a place to secrete her.

THE DUKE

Good. But you will devise a place in the meanwhile.

POLVERINO

My Lord, I will walk about until I have thought
of a place.

THE DUKE

Angela, you have heard us. Not a step until I
return—and not a sound.

ANGELA

[*Clinging to him.*]
Oh, My Lord! Do not leave me here.

THE DUKE

Why not?

ANGELA

I shall be afraid.

THE DUKE

Nonsense. Of what?

ANGELA

Of being alone . . . of the dark.

THE DUKE

She's nervous, Polverino. Where's Emilia? [*Re-membering her departure with horror.*] Good God! She didn't return to the palace?

POLVERINO

I did not see her, My Lord.

THE DUKE

We must find her, or she will give the game away. [*To* ANGELA.] Call her, but not too loud. She may be near.

ANGELA

[*Not too loud.*]
Emilia. Emilia. Come here.

EMILIA

[*Appearing instantly.*]
I'm coming.

THE DUKE

She wasn't a dozen feet away. She's been peeking. But never mind, now. Polverino, I'm relying on you.
[*He goes, and* POLVERINO, *exiting, crosses* EMILIA.]

EMILIA

[*Giggling.*]
I saw the Duke kiss you.

ANGELA

An awful thing's happened. The Duchess has arrived.

EMILIA

[*Seating herself.*]
Was that why the Duke ran away?

ANGELA

He doesn't know what to do.

EMILIA

[*Interested.*]
Are dukes afraid of their wives, too?

ANGELA

If she finds me here . . .
[*They leap to their feet in a panic and clutch
    each other, too alarmed to cry out. A figure
    which, unseen to them, had appeared on top
    of the wall during their brief talk, has half-
    climbed, half-dropped to the ground. It is
    CELLINI, dagger between his teeth; and, re-
    covering his balance, he sees them.*]

CELLINI

[*His dagger in hand, now.*]
Who's there?

EMILIA

Recognizing his voice.]
It's the Master!

CELLINI

Emilia?

ANGELA

You—Benvenuto?

CELLINI

Angela!
[*He takes her in his arms and leads her to the
bench, while* EMILIA *stands uncertainly.*]

ANGELA

[*Recovering from the shock.*]
How did you ever get here?

CELLINI

Through rivers of blood.

ANGELA

I heard the Duke sent soldiers to the house.

CELLINI

I killed them.

ANGELA

Both of them?

CELLINI

Let me tell you about it. I called one of the rogues into the workshop and disposed of him before he had time to draw. Then, I called the other, but he sprang back, when I attacked, and it was nip and tuck for a while. Finally, I managed to poignard him and rip him on the point of my sword, at the same instant! It was a bloody business.

ANGELA

The Duke will never forgive you.

CELLINI

He cannot rob me of these moments with you. I should have slain an army—had one been in my way —to reach your side, tonight.

ANGELA

The Duke forbade you to leave the house.

CELLINI

My heart ordered me to go. [*Notices* EMILIA; *roughly to her.*] Get away from here!

EMILIA

[*She has never affronted him before.*] I won't!

CELLINI

Won't! Do you say won't to me?

EMILIA

[*Weakening.*]
They're always sending me away. . .
[*But she starts to go, rear.*]

ANGELA

[*Detaining her.*]
No. Not there. [*Points, right.*] There. Warn
us if the Duke comes.

EMILIA

[*Loyal, if petulant.*]
Look out for Polverino.
[*Exits, right.*]

CELLINI

[*Savagely.*]
Is Polverino here?

ANGELA

He is walking in the gardens. We must be careful.

CELLINI

He must be careful. [*Not with curiosity, but
anguish.*] Has the Duke made love to you?

ANGELA

He began . . . but he heard that the Duchess had
arrived.

CELLINI

Did he dance a tarantella at the news?

ANGELA

He ran to her.   But he will be back, soon.

CELLINI

Then we will make the most of the little time we
have left.   Oh, my dear Angela!   You cannot imagine my desolation when they took you away.   And
you—were you happy?

ANGELA

[*Pausing.*]
I was very happy in your house.

CELLINI

Let us be happy here.   Let us forget all that we
can of trouble and remember all that we can of joy.
See, how black it is everywhere! yet to me, these
moments are white butterflies, perfuming the way to
the Unknown . . . And look: there is a rose; now,
look deeper and farther, look into my heart, and see
the rose you have set there.

ANGELA

[*Nestling to him.*]
I wish that the Duke weren't coming back.

CELLINI

Believe me, he is not coming back.

ANGELA

He promised.

CELLINI

He cannot come back; he is far behind us; he cannot touch us. Life has begun from a new, safe source, and all things flow from the future. We are here, hands held, lips pressed . . . [*a lengthy kiss*] forever.

ANGELA

[*Dreamily.*]
Ah! The Duke used that word.

CELLINI

[*Disconcerted.*]
Did he get that far? . . . But do not mention the Duke; how can I think of the Duke when I can only think of you? The Duke is the world, and the world has vanished; it was a bad dream of last night, gone in the dawning light of you. What is everything? I divide the heavens, I count the suns, I multiply the stars, and add them all up to—you.

ANGELA

[*Softly.*]
I should like to learn . . . to love you.

CELLINI

My words are your tutors.

ANGELA

I should like to want you . . . when you are away.

CELLINI

Listen: I have been away for an eternity. Day after day you have climbed to the top of the tall hill, hoping in vain to see me come down the long, long road. And now—at last—you see me. You wave your shawl. You cannot wait for me to reach you, so long is the road, so wild is your pulse! You race as fast as your little feet will carry you . . . you reach me—and throw your arms around me—and now you have caught me in the net of your wonder!

ANGELA

[*Half-stirred.*]
And would you do anything for me?

CELLINI

Anything.

ANGELA

[*Thinking of something for him to do.*]
Then make me a ring like you made for the Duchess!

CELLINI

[*A little jarred by her instant reaction.*]

You are quick to follow me up. But to be at your feet is to be above thrones.

ANGELA

And you will always think of me?

CELLINI

Always.

ANGELA

You wouldn't leave me . . . for another?

CELLINI

Never.

ANGELA

[*Probing further.*]
You wouldn't leave me . . . if I wanted you with me . . . for your work?

CELLINI

[*Unthinkingly.*]
Never. [*He realizes the meaning of her words.*] My work! Did you say my work?
[*Abruptly releases her and is on his feet.*]

ANGELA

[*Looking left and right, anxiously.*]
Is someone coming?

CELLINI

[*Beating his breast.*]
How the devil should I know?

ANGELA

[*Uncomprehendingly.*]
Then what is it?

CELLINI

[*Unaware of her presence.*]
The Cardinal's cup! I left it on the anvil—they
will steal my beautiful cup! O Lord, don't let them
steal my cup—it isn't finished.

ANGELA

[*Humbly.*]
Benvenuto! You forget me.

CELLINI

[*Returning to himself.*]
Forget you? Never. You are always first in my
thoughts.

ANGELA

[*Commandingly.*]
Then sit by me.

CELLINI

[*Unheeding her, groaning.*]
That damned Ottaviano! I think he has made me
forget the design for the Atlas . . .

ANGELA

[*Not humbly.*]
Benvenuto!

CELLINI

Silence.   Ah! it was to have been a figure, engraved
on a plate of gold . . .

ANGELA

I'll go away!

CELLINI

. . . the ·heaven on its back was a crystal ball,
on which was cut the Zodiac . . .

ANGELA

I'll never speak to you again!

CELLINI

. . . on a field of lapis-lazuli!
[EMILIA *enters in haste.*]

EMILIA

The Duke is coming.

CELLINI

[*Out of his trance.*]
The Duke?   I must see him.

ANGELA

It will be terrible if he finds you with me.

CELLINI

You are right. He will not give me a chance to explain. He must be told that I am here . . . that I have information of the greatest importance. Angela—but I cannot bear the thought of leaving you . . . not even for a few minutes.

ANGELA

For my sake, you must.

CELLINI

I will hide. You must tell him that I am here. Cajole him to see me; say that. . . Yes, say that I know of a plot against his life.

ANGELA

I dare not.

EMILIA

[*At the extreme right.*]
He is getting close.

ANGELA

[*Ready to promise everything.*]
I will, I will!

EMILIA

[*Excitedly.*]
Go! Go! He is here.
    [CELLINI *leaps over the wall.* EMILIA *joins*

Angela. *They sit in silence. The* Duke *enters.*]

THE DUKE

[*Pausing as he enters.*]
Angela! I thought I'd never get back.

ANGELA

You were long, Your Excellency.

THE DUKE

[*Gallantly.*]
It was longer for me. And fancy . . . [*Moves towards the bench*] she only wanted to see me to say, good night. [*Spies* Emilia; *pettishly.*] Go away from here.

EMILIA

Go where, My Lord?

THE DUKE

Oh, go to America. Climb a tree or fall down a well—it's all the same to me. But go away. And don't peek this time, as you did before.

EMILIA

No, My Lord.
[*Exits, left.*]

THE DUKE

Isn't it outrageous, what a time a man in my position has to get alone with a girl?

ANGELA

I have something to tell you, My Lord.

THE DUKE

[*Rebuking her.*]
We are alone.

ANGELA

Bumpy—it's about Cellini, Bumpy.

THE DUKE

I forbid you to mention his name.   Talk about me.

ANGELA

But it is very important.

THE DUKE

So am I.   No more of this now.

ANGELA

[*Pleadingly.*]
But Bumpy——

OTTAVIANO'S VOICE

[*Off right, interrupting her.*]
Alessandro!   Alessandro!

THE DUKE

[*Supremely vexed.*]
Are we never to be left alone?

OTTAVIANO'S VOICE

[*Approaching.*]
Alessandro!

THE DUKE

And my own cousin, too.   One would think that at
least he would have some consideration.

[*Enter* OTTAVIANO, *and soldiers bearing lan-
terns.*]

OTTAVIANO

[*Agitated.*]
Is that you, Alessandro?

THE DUKE

No, it isn't.   And if it is, I am busy.

OTTAVIANO

I have the gravest news.

THE DUKE

It will wait until tomorrow.

OTTAVIANO

Cellini has escaped.   ·

THE DUKE

Then order the soldiers to catch him and let me alone.

OTTAVIANO

He plots against your life.

THE DUKE

Plots against my life! [*To* ANGELA.] Then that's what you wanted to tell me.

ANGELA

[*Overwhelmed.*]
I know nothing, Bumpy.

THE DUKE

[*Whispering.*]
Not in public, I said.

OTTAVIANO

I know everything. When I stayed behind to instruct Cellini on the reverse for the medal, he proposed to me that it would be to our mutual advantage if you were put out of the way, Alessandro.

THE DUKE

So it would be. What did you say?

OTTAVIANO

I led him on and told him I would return later to discuss the details. When I arrived, I found that he had killed his guard and fled.

THE DUKE

[*Irritated by the entire proceeding.*]
He might have waited a day. I had planned such an enjoyable evening.

OTTAVIANO

[*Displaying his impatience.*]
Alessandro, it would be best if you gave orders to hang him directly he is caught.

THE DUKE

[*Feebly assuming the ducal air.*]
We order that Cellini be hanged directly that he is caught and give the matter into your hands for execution. [*Relapsing into his mood.*] And now, go away.

OTTAVIANO

[*To the soldiers.*]
A hundred ducats to the man who brings me Cellini dead!
[*A piercing scream is heard.*]

THE DUKE

What was that?

OTTAVIANO

[*Staring into the dark.*]
That was murder.

A SOLDIER

Someone is coming, My Lord!
[*They grasp their weapons.* POLVERINO *staggers in, rear, and almost falls; the* SOLDIER *catches him.*]

OTTAVIANO

It is Polverino.   He is wounded.

THE DUKE

Polverino?   Wounded?   In my grounds?

POLVERINO

[*Gasping.*]
My Lord . . . I am dead.

OTTAVIANO

[*Scenting his prey.*]
Who has killed you?

POLVERINO

Cellini.

THE DUKE

[*Showing fear.*]
Cellini here?

POLVERINO

I stumbled across him. . . I am dead.
[*Collapses in the* SOLDIER'S *arms.*]

THE DUKE

Treason!

OTTAVIANO

[*Swiftly.*]
Two hundred ducats to the man who brings me
Cellini dead!
[*General excitement, as the soldiers and* OT-
TAVIANO *exit.* POLVERINO *has been rudely
laid on the earth.*]

THE DUKE

[*Calling after them.*]
Beat the bushes! Don't let him escape! I won't
feel comfortable until he's hanged.

ANGELA

[*Swooning.*]
My Lord . . . I am unwell.

THE DUKE

Good heavens! You mustn't do that here! They shouldn't have left me alone. Angela . . . wake up, like a good little girl. . . What will I do with her? Polverino! Why don't you answer me? What will I do with her? [*Leans* ANGELA *against back of the bench and goes to* POLVERINO. *Shakes him.*] Polverino! You must speak. What will I do with her? Where will I take her?

POLVERINO

[*Murmuring, as the* DUKE *raises him.*]
To your own room. . . The Duchess . . . will never think . . .
[*Falls back, unconscious again.*]

THE DUKE

[*Dropping him.*]
To my own room! The Duchess will never think! . . . Oh, Polverino! What a clever servant I have lost in you. [*Goes to* ANGELA, *endeavors to arouse her.*] Angela!

ANGELA

[*Opening her eyes.*]
I am . . . so cold. . . .

THE DUKE

[*Jubilantly.*]

She's coming to! . . . Angela, try to walk. [*He supports her as they move right. At the exit, he turns and shouts.*] Find him! Hang him! [*To the fallen courtier.*] Polverino— Oh, he's dead.

    [*Half carries her off, right.*]

        [CELLINI *vaults back over the wall, and hearing a noise, crouches behind a rosebush. Two soldiers cross from left to right in search of him.* EMILIA *comes in with a thousand horrid shapes about her.*]

EMILIA

[*To the bench.*]

Angela! My Lord! What's happened? Oh! I'm so scared.

    [*She sees* POLVERINO'S *body, and runs off, left, screaming.* ASCANIO *drops over the wall.*]

ASCANIO

Emilia! Emilia! Emilia!

    [*He rushes out, rear.*]

OTTAVIANO'S VOICE

[*Wrathfully, off right.*]

He's somewhere around here! He must be found. Look for him, I tell you. Find him—find him.

CELLINI

[*Emerging and going right.*]

There is one place they will not look for me—in the Duchess's bed. . . .

[*He runs off.*]

[*The scene is blotted out, for the moon has suddenly gone down. It rises again, in a few minutes, on a corner of the Palace's balcony. To the front is a low, white stone railing; behind it, the rather broad balcony; and then, the Palace itself, in obscurity. The light falls somewhat to the right, revealing two large curtained, glass doors, side by side; the first opens into the* DUCHESS'S *room, the other into the* DUKE'S. *These doors swing respectively right and left, so that when they are opened, the space between them is unobstructed, as now, when they are closed. The light falls brightest on this spot, and slopes away to the left, dimly revealing where the balcony turns with the building. Beyond this, left, and below everywhere, the night is unbroken. Thus,* CELLINI *is not seen as he climbs to the balcony just where it turns, right, but is visible as soon as he surmounts the railing. With the utmost caution, he makes his way over it, and to the* DUCHESS'S *door. Here, he stops and listens; takes the key which he has; fits it into the lock as quietly as possible; turns it, and slowly, very slowly, pulls out the door. The room is in darkness, save for one candle. This is held by the* DUCHESS, *who has heard him and stands on the threshold in négligée. Throughout the scene all talk is pianissimo.*]

THE DUCHESS

Cellini?

CELLINI

My Lady . . . let me in.

THE DUCHESS

[*Stepping on to the balcony.*]
You are impatient, now, who were so slow before.

CELLINI

My Lady, someone may see us, here.

THE DUCHESS

[*Stepping on to the balcony.*]
We are safer here than in my room. The Duke sleeps next door.

CELLINI

You are daring, Madam.

THE DUCHESS

What woman would not be daring when the moon shines? What a beautiful evening, Benvenuto.

CELLINI

Beautiful with your presence, My Lady.

THE DUCHESS

The night is our friend. You may take my hand, Benvenuto. [*He kisses her hand, she sighs.*] Now, we three together, holding hands—you, and I, and the night.

CELLINI

Madam, you make me jealous of the night.

THE DUCHESS

You are ardent, now, who were so . . . honorable, before. I wondered if you would come.

CELLINI

[*Boastfully.*]
I came, although the Duke had my house guarded.

THE DUCHESS

And you did this . . .

CELLINI

[*Giving language to her implication.*]
To reach you, My Lady. Nothing could have stood in my way.

THE DUCHESS

Nothing?

CELLINI

I would have killed an army to be with you, to-night.

THE DUCHESS

And for the joy I will give you, it would not have been too much.

CELLINI

There is more than you have heard.

THE DUCHESS

More of danger?

CELLINI

Polverino saw me, in the gardens. I had to stab him.

THE DUCHESS

Do not mourn for him.

CELLINI

[*Dryly.*]
I do not, Madam.

THE DUCHESS

I knew him well. He was a wretch.

CELLINI

I do not mourn for him, but for myself—when the Duke hears of these things.

THE DUCHESS

Do not be afraid. I will tell you a secret. . . You think me the Duchess?

CELLINI

My Lady, surely.

THE DUCHESS

[*Charmingly.*]
I am not. I am the Duke.

CELLINI

I ask pardon, for my crimes, from Your Lordship.

THE DUCHESS

With my lips, I pardon you.
[*They kiss.*]

CELLINI

Ah, Madam! You will drive me on to more crimes.

THE DUCHESS

Why will I do that? . . . Do not think that I do
not know your answer, but it will be pleasant to hear,
even so.

CELLINI

You will drive me to commit more crimes . . .
that I may receive more pardons.

THE DUCHESS

You do not have to wait. I will give you absolu-
tion for all your crimes of the future.
[*They kiss, again.*]

CELLINI

[*Apparently inflamed.*]
My Lady, let us go inside.

THE DUCHESS

[*With a little laugh.*]
I believe that you are a man, after all.

CELLINI

Polverino will swear to it, in Hell.

THE DUCHESS

[*Wickedly.*]
I hope to swear to it, on Earth.

CELLINI

Do not let us delay longer, Madam.

THE DUCHESS

You are too much in haste.

CELLINI

When I killed Polverino, he aroused the guard.
They searched for me, in the gardens. I may be
seen.

THE DUCHESS

The guard passed you?

CELLINI

Yes, but they will return, Madam.

THE DUCHESS

They will never dream of seeing you on my balcony, and if they do, they will think it is the Duke.
There is no danger.

CELLINI

[*His pride wounded.*]
You wrong me, Madam.

THE DUCHESS

Not willingly, my Benvenuto.

CELLINI

It is not for fear of them, but for love of you,
that I would withdraw.

THE DUCHESS

[*Offering her mouth.*]
Now, it is you who must pardon me.
[*They kiss, passionately.*]

CELLINI

[*Taking advantage of her closed eyes to look
about for enemies.*]
My Lady——

THE DUCHESS

[*A gentle interruption.*]
When our lips met, I was no longer your Lady, but
your love.

CELLINI

My love! . . Let us go. See: it is not only
your soldiers' eyes that watch us.

THE DUCHESS

The night has eyes, too.

CELLINI

[*Ruefully.*]
A thousand eyes!

THE DUCHESS

And my room . . . has none.

CELLINI

We will leave the night behind, and take its brilliance with us.

THE DUCHESS

[*Laughing strangely.*]
You are too much in a hurry.

CELLINI

My heart races to be with you—alone.

THE DUCHESS

I weave a laurel for your sure victory.

CELLINI

My blood is red, but you are in my blood like a redder poppy.

THE DUCHESS

Let me flower there a little before you pluck me.

CELLINI

You are not a woman: you are a torch.

THE DUCHESS

[*Thrillingly.*]
We shall have light in our dark room.

CELLINI

I am on fire.

THE DUCHESS

Press me close, that I may catch the delicious flame.

CELLINI

I used your key to open your door, let me use it, now, to lock your door!

THE DUCHESS

[*Not meaning it.*]
You must be patient.

CELLINI

Was Paris patient in Helen's arms?

THE DUCHESS

And for his haste, he was killed. Let us hold on to these sweet moments until the sweet becomes unbearable. . . .

CELLINI

Beauty's mother was cruelty.

THE DUCHESS

But her child is kindness, as you will live to learn tonight. [*Disengaging herself as much as* CELLINI *will permit.*] I must leave you, for an instant.

CELLINI

Cannot we go together?

THE DUCHESS

I must see that the Duke is in his room, that he sleeps.

CELLINI

[*Releasing her.*]
Well, I trust.

THE DUCHESS

[*Taking the candle.*]
Better than we shall sleep. . .
[*She brings the door forward with her; they embrace in its shadow; she goes, and* CELLINI *shuts the door.*]

CELLINI

[*With a gesture of repugnance.*]
It was Angela that I was kissing!
[*He has taken a few steps left, and turns to see the* DUKE's *door opening. With a bound, he vanishes around the corner of the terrace, where he is effectively lost in the gloom. The door swings wider, and the* DUKE *and* ANGELA *emerge. She is dressed as before, but her hair has fallen. It is evident that she has not yet recovered from her swoon; the* DUKE *assists her.*]

THE DUKE

[*Cheerfully.*]

Since lying down didn't help you, I'm sure that the air will. You'll be yourself in no time.

ANGELA

[*Supporting herself on the rail.*]
You are very good, My Lord.

THE DUKE

Not at all—I expect that someone would do as much for me, if I were sick.

ANGELA

We may be seen.

THE DUKE

We are safer here than in my room. [*Points.*]
The Duchess sleeps there.

ANGELA

[*Shivering.*]
I am afraid.

THE DUKE

Nonsense. The only danger was in getting you by.

ANGELA

But the Duchess may awake.

THE DUKE

She retired as soon as she arrived. I'm sure that
she's snoring—she always does. As long as we
don't talk too loud, we're absolutely all right. [*Re-
coils.*] What was that?

ANGELA

[*Ready to faint again.*]
Someone is knocking.

THE DUKE

Hush!
  [*The knocking—a very soft one,—is heard
  again.*]

ANGELA

It's at your door.

THE DUKE

[*Ready to faint himself.*]
Don't I know it? . . . I'll pretend to be asleep.
  [*The* DUCHESS *is heard calling "Alessandro,"
  in a voice calculated not to arouse him if he
  is asleep.*]

ANGELA

Hadn't you better answer her?

THE DUKE

How should I know? If only Polverino were

here. . . Oh! I left the door unlocked, she may
come in! Wait. I'll speak to her, and listen until
she's back in her room.

> [*He goes.* ANGELA *closes the door behind him,
> and leans weakly against it.* CELLINI *comes
> out of his refuge and tiptoes towards her.*]

CELLINI

Angela!

ANGELA

[*Astonished.*]
Benvenuto!
[*Droops into his arms.*]

CELLINI

[*Fiercely.*]
What has happened?

ANGELA

I am afraid.

CELLINI

Of the Duke?

ANGELA

Of the Duchess. I like the Duke.

CELLINI

[*Jealous.*]
You must hate the Duke and love me.

ANGELA

Oh! You were plotting to kill him, weren't you?

CELLINI

[*Divining a fresh misfortune.*]
Who said that?

ANGELA

Ottaviano told the Duke so.

CELLINI

[*Taut, to himself.*]
This time, there is no escape.

ANGELA

[*Hopefully.*]
Were you going to kill him . . . for me?

CELLINI

[*Crushing her in his arms, in pain.*]
For you, and for no one else! Angela! Hark!
Do you hear those bells?

ANGELA

I hear no bells.

CELLINI

[*Tenderly.*]
They ring over my own Summer Palace.

ANGELA

[*Decisively.*]
You haven't one.

CELLINI

[*Lifting her from the ground.*]
Oh, Angela, Angela, you are my Summer Palace,
my house under the stars, and every star a silver
bell which rings, come home, come home!

ANGELA

[*As he starts right with her.*]
But the Duke. . . .

CELLINI

[*Pausing.*]
What is a Duke compared to Cellini? Tomorrow
my life ends, but tonight I find endless life. [*With
sudden sadness.*] Summer is almost over, and
already there is a chill in the air. . . [*With as
sudden exaltation.*] But tonight is Spring, and the
colors and fires of Spring!

ANGELA

[*Alarmed and delighted.*]
Where are we going?

CELLINI

[*Reckless, with a great laugh.*]

Where are we not going!   [*Starts right again.*]
There are no blossoms we shall not touch, no heavens
we shall not see!

ANGELA

[*As he throws a leg over the rail.*]
I will fall.

CELLINI

Hold on to my heart, and fly.

ANGELA

[*Holds on not to his heart, but his neck.*]
Aren't you afraid of what the Duke will do?

CELLINI

[*Triumphantly, as he throws his other leg
over.*]

Let him howl—tonight another thief enters into
Paradise!

> [*Darkness swallows them as they disappear
> below the edge of the balcony. Simultane-
> ously, both doors open, and the* DUKE *and
> the* DUCHESS, *each bearing a candle, step
> out. As they become aware of each other,
> the* DUCHESS *gives only a slight indication
> of the shock; but the* DUKE *narrowly avoids*

apoplexy. The DUCHESS *imagines that* CEL-
LINI *is hidden behind her door; the* DUKE
imagines that ANGELA *is hidden behind his
door. Instinctively, she looks right and he,
left. There is a silent moment of vast relief
for both. Then . . .*]

THE DUCHESS

[*Coldly.*]
A lovely evening, my Lord.

THE DUKE

[*Stuttering.*]
A lovely evening, Madam.
[*They diligently study the skies.*]

ACT III

The workshop, again, late next morning.
CELLINI, *hammer and chisel at hand, is at the
anvil.* ANGELA *sits near, but a different* AN-
GELA *than she who drooped in* CELLINI'S *arms.
There has been a subtle change in her de-
meanor; she is neither as shy nor as humble as
she was, but a good deal more self-assured. . . .
Her face wears an inquisitive expression.*

CELLINI
[*Turning on her with the voice of a man who
has endured all that he can possibly stand.*]
For heaven's sake, stop your talking and leave me
alone!

ANGELA
[*Sullenly.*]
I won't!

CELLINI
[*With obvious self-control.*]
I must finish this cup.

ANGELA
[*Boldly.*]
I don't want you to finish it.

156

CELLINI

[*Wearily.*]

I've explained, often enough, that I have only a few hours of life left. . . .

ANGELA

[*Sniffing.*]

You just say that to make me feel bad.

CELLINI

. . . and that I must get through as much work as I can.

ANGELA

I don't want you to work.

CELLINI

[*Looking at her oddly.*]

I am beginning to realize that.

ANGELA

When you work, you forget all about me. [*With a quick smile.*] I want you to sit with me.

CELLINI

[*Brutally.*]

What for?

ANGELA

[*In a little temper of her own.*]

So that you can talk to me—that's what for!

CELLINI

[*Hammering savagely.*]
I talked to you for two hours, this morning.

ANGELA

Talk to me some more.

CELLINI

You did nothing but repeat yourself.

ANGELA

[*Hurt.*]
You treat me as if I were a child.

CELLINI

[*Feeling that he has been offensive.*]
I don't mean to treat you that way, my dear child.

ANGELA

[*Seizing her advantage.*]
Then come over here.

CELLINI

[*With an impotent gesture.*]
What do you want of me?
[*Goes to her.*]

ANGELA

[*Making room for him on her chair.*]
Sit here.

CELLINI

[*Sitting; half good-naturedly.*]
There! Now are you happy?
[*Stares miserably towards the anvil.*]

ANGELA

[*Cooing.*]
Not yet. [*Places his arm around her waist.*}
Now!

CELLINI

[*After a pause.*]
How much longer am I supposed to do this?

ANGELA

[*Definitely.*]
Until I tell you not to.

CELLINI

[*After another pause.*]
Angela . . . I worship the ground you walk on
—but I must get to work.

ANGELA

[*Drawing his arm tighter.*]
You think more of your work than you do of me!

CELLINI

[*Nonplussed, since this is true.*]
You don't understand.

ANGELA

Dear Benvenuto, you must promise me something.

CELLINI

[*Suspiciously.*]
Promise you what?

ANGELA

[*With little amatory tricks.*]
Never, unless I say "yes" . . . to do any work!

CELLINI

[*Revolting.*]
I'm damned if I makc that promise.

ANGELA

[*Putting her fingers over his mouth.*]
And never to use bad language before me.

CELLINI

[*Furious, then apologetic.*]
I can't help it!—now and then.

ANGELA

And always to love me . . .

CELLINI

[*Softening.*]
I promise that.

ANGELA

—as you did last night . . .

CELLINI

[*Seduced.*]
Ah! last night.

ANGELA

—in the darkness . . .

CELLINI

[*Rapturously.*]
There was no darkness, last night; there was a
flame. I think that I shall never burn with that
flame again; night reveals its secret fire only once.

ANGELA

I made you happy.

CELLINI

Happy? Do not use that melancholy word, Angela. Love begins where happiness ends.

ANGELA

I made you happy. Will you make me happy?

CELLINI

[*Unsuspiciously.*]
I will do my best, Angela.

ANGELA

[*Swiftly.*]
Then promise you won't work this morning!

CELLINI

[*Tearing himself loose, violently.*]
A fine snare! Your mother named you Angela,
but you were named Lillith before you were born.
What has come over you, since yesterday?

ANGELA

You told me that I must live, as if I were real.
Since I have heard that my mother is dead, and since
I knew that a Duke could desire me, and since you
told me that you would have killed him, for me. . . .

CELLINI

What of it?

ANGELA

I feel different. I feel more than I did like telling
people to do things for me.

CELLINI

[*Angrily.*]
Well, tell people, but don't tell me. Once and
for all, I tell you not to disturb me.

ANGELA

You don't love me.

CELLINI

A woman says that when she wants a man to hate himself forever.

ANGELA

The Duke would not treat me so.

CELLINI

[*Enraged by the name.*]
Then go to him!

ANGELA

[*Indignantly.*]
I won't! You took me away, and now you'll have to keep me. [*Breaking down.*] Go to the Duke! I said that you didn't love me.

CELLINI

[*Feeling that he has gone too far.*]
I didn't really mean for you to go to the Duke.

ANGELA

You want me to play second fiddle to a furnace.

CELLINI

[*Perplexed.*]
Believe me, I do not. You come before everything.

ANGELA

If I do, you'll sit with me again.

CELLINI

[*Surrendering.*]
It is silly of us to quarrel, when I am so near the gallows.

ANGELA

[*Confident.*]
I will save you.

CELLINI

[*Skeptical.*]
You?

ANGELA

The Duke likes me.

CELLINI

[*His blood freezing.*]
What are you thinking?

ANGELA

He will do anything for me . . . if I am kind to him.

CELLINI

[*Shouting.*]
I forbid you to dream of it! [*In a more normal tone.*] I had rather go to Hell after I am dead, than before.

ANGELA

But I do not want you to die. And what will be the difference?

CELLINI

[*Stupefied by her insensitiveness.*]
The difference? Will you feel none?

ANGELA

Why should I?

CELLINI

[*Staggered.*]
Why should you? [*Shaking her.*]
Don't you love me?

ANGELA

You're hurting me.

CELLINI

[*Quieting his hands.*]
Don't you love me?

ANGELA

That is why I should do it!

CELLINI

[*Laughing wildly.*]
Oh, that's why!

ANGELA

[*Missing his irony.*]
Of course, and it isn't as if I didn't like him.

CELLINI

[*Madly hilarious.*]
Nothing like it!

ANGELA

Then you'll let me save you?

CELLINI

[*Losing all his mirth; sternly.*]
No. Put the Duke out of your head.

ANGELA

But he will kill you!

CELLINI

My faith is in my God. He knows that I am a
man of peace, beset by villainous trouble-makers. He
will not fail me.

ANGELA

But the Duke has given Ottaviano orders to hang
you.

CELLINI

And here I am wasting the minutes!
[*Turns resolutely to the anvil.*]

ANGELA

[*Pleadingly.*]
Benvenuto.

CELLINI

[*Sharply.*]
Find something around the house to clean.

ANGELA

[*Mournfully.*]
Last night you told me that you would never
let me soil my white hands. . . .

CELLINI

[*At work.*]
It was very silly of me.
  [BEATRICE *appears at the left front door, very
      much alive; but she uses a cane to aid her
      walk.*]

ANGELA

[*Her back to* BEATRICE.]
It wasn't silly. I want you to talk to me.

BEATRICE

[*Raising her stick.*]
I'll talk to you—with this!

ANGELA

[*Terrorized, retreats to* CELLINI.]
It's my mother. Don't let her beat me.

BEATRICE

[*Enters, ignoring* CELLINI.]

I knew that I'd find you here! I told the Duke, last night, before I took on so.

ANGELA

[*Clinging to* CELLINI]
Don't let her come any nearer.

CELLINI

[*Flashing his chisel at* BEATRICE.]
Shall I carve you a new face? [BEATRICE *stops still.*] You could use a new one, you know.

BEATRICE

Kidnaper! Home-wrecker!

CELLINI

[*Impatiently.*]
What do you want?

BEATRICE

My forty ducats.

CELLINI

[*Surprised.*]
Forty ducats?

BEATRICE

For my daughter.

CELLINI

[*Turning to work again.*]
Don't be a fool. You gave her to the Duke.

BEATRICE

[*Choking.*]
You stole her away.

CELLINI

[*Hammering.*]
She came with me, of her own accord.

BEATRICE

She never did! . . . If you don't give me my
forty ducats, I'll take her away.

CELLINI

[*Seeing a ray of light.*]
Take her away? By all means.

BEATRICE

[*Unexpectedly.*]
You can't make me take her away.

CELLINI

It was your idea.

BEATRICE

You can't make me take her away. I want my
forty ducats.

CELLINI

[*Pausing, politely.*]

My dear lady, you agreed to give Angela to me, and then gave her to the Duke instead. Consequently, I owe you nothing.

BEATRICE

But the Duke may not have her, now.

CELLINI

[*Resuming his labors.*]

That would be a pity.

BEATRICE

[*Pointing out her whole misfortune.*]

I may lose him . . . and the forty ducats, too.

CELLINI

[*Cheerfully.*] Life is hard.

BEATRICE

[*Frantically.*]

You give me forty ducats.

CELLINI

Beatrice, you are making me very tired. If you don't get out of here——

BEATRICE

[*Choking anew.*]

If you don't give me the forty ducats, I'll take on again, as I did last night. I'll have a stroke, I will, right here.

CELLINI

[*Whistling.*]

Don't let me interfere with your pleasures.

BEATRICE

[*To* ANGELA.]

You! Make him give me my money!

ANGELA

[*Gathering her courage.*]

I won't. . . . You scared me when you came in because I thought you were dead.

BEATRICE

[*To* CELLINI.]

Just like I said yesterday; you've turned my own daughter against me. I'm a respectable woman, and if you don't give me my money, I'll have the law on you.

CELLINI

[*Amused.*]

They're going to hang me, today.

[*A knocking at the rear door.* CELLINI, *nervously.*]
Who's there?

PIER'S VOICE

Benvenuto.
    [CELLINI *goes to the door.*]

BEATRICE

[*Spitefully.*]
Next time it'll be the hangman.
    [CELLINI *has admitted* PIER, *and is shutting
        the door.   He turns furiously on* BEATRICE,
        who retreats left front.]

CELLINI

[*Pushes her bodily through the exit.*]
Out, witch, out!

BEATRICE

[*Unseen.*]
I'll stay to see you strung up!

ANGELA

[*Sulking, as he turns towards her.*]
I suppose you want me to go, too.

CELLINI

I must see Pier alone, Angela.

ANGELA

[*Bitingly.*]
Oh, very well.
[*She goes right front.*]

CELLINI

[*Eagerly.*]
You told the Duke I was here?

PIER

[*Gravely.*]
What have you done to the Duchess?

CELLINI

You saw her?

PIER

Saw her? I heard her. I thought I could count
on her, and found her more set against you than
the Duke himself.

CELLINI

What did the Duke say, when he learned I was
here?

PIER

That you were crazy, or you would not have sent
me to tell him; for he will certainly hang you before
the morning is over.

CELLINI

Ottaviano has done his work well. Did you see
the Duchess alone?

PIER

She will be here directly.

CELLINI

Then I am saved!

PIER

I would not be too sure. She gave me this message: "Tell Cellini that I come, but that the gallows follow me."

CELLI

[*Swaggering.*]
The Duke was about.

PIER

The Duke had gone.

CELLINI

[*Crestfallen.*]
Then her anger was real.

PIER

Real? You should have been there! She was not human—she was a woman carved in ice.

CELLINI

[*Thoughtfully.*]
Nevertheless, she comes here. . . .

PIER

Benvenuto, what have you done to the lady?
She was always your friend.

CELLINI

I designed a ring which she disliked.

PIER

An odd reason for wishing a man strangled.

CELLINI

If ever I get out of this scrape, I will never look
at another woman.

PIER

[*Slyly.*]

It occurred to me . . . that perhaps you had not
looked at the Duchess?

CELLINI

Perhaps not! and I wish that I had never looked
at any other beside her. When you were here earlier, I did not tell you that I have Angela with me.

PIER

Angela? I saw her last night with the Duke, in
the gardens.

CELLINI

I stole her.

PIER

Then you are dead. The Duke will forgive murder, but not the loss of a girl.

CELLINI

[*Dejectedly.*]

I stole her! And what have I found? That what was rich and mystical under the stars, was gross and common in the light of day.

PIER

That discovery is generally made at twenty.

CELLINI

You have no idea of the change in her! Yesterday she was mute; I had to drag the syllables from her, almost by force!

PIER

And today she chatters away like the teeth of a coward.

CELLINI

How did you know?

PIER

Experience, my young friend, has taught me that love is quiet, and domestic life is noisy.

CELLINI

Yesterday, when I was near, she was pale, and

kept her eyes on the ground; today she orders me to do this and not to do that, as if I were her lackey!

PIER

Do you obey her?

CELLINI

I rage—and find myself doing as she tells me! I will never have any peace of mind, while she is in the house.

PIER

You don't love her.

CELLINI

You take the words from her mouth!—I don't know; yesterday, I would have sworn. . .

PIER

Yesterday, she was remote, and the Duke's; today she is near, and yours! Surely, a man of thirty-five should have learned that what are flowers from afar, are thorns in the hand, and that to reach the Promised Land, is to lose it.

CELLINI

[*Sadly.*]

Happy the traveler, then, who never sights his home!

PIER

But you have never loved Angela.

CELLINI

Inexpressibly. The thought of her awoke things within me . . . like the most delicate petals, trembling in the wind, glowing in the light of her. . .

PIER

In the beginning, she was the merest rag-doll: Your imagination seized upon her; shaped her into a mystery, enveloped her in magic, and painted her in celestial colors! but the mystery, the magic, and the colors were your own. They belonged to her, only as you lent them to her. And now—your eyes have swept clear what your fancy painted; and after all, she is only a poor, human thing.

CELLINI

That girl is a greater menace to me than the Duke.

PIER

Be kind: do not blame her for your own mistake. But do not sacrifice yourself: that would be a greater mistake. However, you wouldn't; sacrifice isn't in your nature.

CELLINI

[*Indignantly.*]

I have been very good to my sister and to her children!

[*A rapid knocking on the rear door.*]

PIER

The Duchess! You will not want me here.

CELLINI

[*Going to the door.*]
Stay in the house.

PIER

[PIER *exits left front. The* DUCHESS *enters,
unaccompanied, and acknowledges* CELLINI'S
*low bow with a stony stare. He closes the
door.*]

CELLINI

[*Rushing towards her.*]
My love!

THE DUCHESS

[*"Carved in ice".*]
Your Lady.

CELLINI

[*Apparently thunderstruck.*]
My Lady? I don't understand.

THE DUCHESS

[*Suspiciously.*]
Didn't your friend convey my message?

CELLINI

[*Assuming a puzzled formality.*]
He did, My Lady.

THE DUCHESS

And you have the impudence! . . .

CELLINI

[*Anger creeping into his address.*]

I thought your message a gesture of protection
for both of us. I see it was not.

THE DUCHESS

[*One foot beating a tattoo.*]

Presently, you will see more.

CELLINI

[*Aggressively.*]

I do see more, Madam. I see that it ill befits a
great lady to make a poor sculptor the butt of her
idle caprices!

THE DUCHESS

[*Thunderstruck in turn.*]

My caprices?

CELLINI

But the fault is my own, My Lady.

THE DUCHESS

[*Breathing hard.*]

It is very good of you to acknowledge it.

CELLINI

[*Lashing out.*]

I should never have been fool enough to believe that Your Ladyship would really condescend to me.

THE DUCHESS
[*Who had expected a suppliant.*]
What game is this that you play?

CELLINI
Game, Madam? I must thank you for supplying the right word: I should have understood that a poor sculptor is fair game for a Duchess.

THE DUCHESS
[*Studying him.*]
You are not only a villain, Cellini, but a clever villain. You try to put me on the defensive. You will not succeed.

CELLINI
Madam, whatever you speak from, I speak from the heart.

THE DUCHESS
[*Biting her lips.*]
You have no heart!

CELLINI
No, for Your Ladyship has torn it out of my breast and flung it in my face!

THE DUCHESS
[*Beating a tattoo again.*]

Cellini, you have my key. I want it. [*He does not look at her as he hands it to her.*] You will have no further use for it.

CELLINI

Madam, then, has finished her sport.

THE DUCHESS

[*Losing ground with her temper.*]
How dare you say that to me? You, who made a fool of me, last night.

CELLINI

Madam has made a fool of me for a lifetime.

THE DUCHESS

[*Her voice revealing her weakening.*]
You left me waiting up for you, like an idiot, until dawn came.

CELLINI

[*Whose one fear was that she knew of* ANGELA.]
Is that all? . . .

THE DUCHESS

[*Witheringly.*]
All?

CELLINI

I spoke unthinkingly, my lady.

THE DUCHESS

Why did you not return? I left you for a moment,
and you were gone for the night.

CELLINI

I could have returned, Madam. But I did not
desire Ottaviano and the executioner for my companions.

THE DUCHESS

What do you mean?

CELLINI

Let me tell you all about it.

THE DUCHESS

I know your tongue: it is as glib as your chisel.

CELLINI

Judge for yourself, Madam. When the Duke
appeared, I vaulted the wall and crouched there.
You left me with my blood in fever, and my one
desire was to reach you again. But Fate does not
grant us bliss, easily. I was seen and chased by the
soldiers.

THE DUCHESS

The Duke and I stood on the balcony for the longest time: It is strange that we heard no noise.

CELLINI

It is not strange, Madam, for I tried to make no noise, and the soldiers did the same. It was hide-and-seek in the dark, and I was It. One fellow caught me, but I laid him out with one blow, before he could yell! Finally, after a dozen hair-breadth escapes, I reached the road. But so great was my desire to be with you—that here, where I was safe, I turned back.

THE DUCHESS

That was bravely done . . . Benvenuto.

CELLINI

[*Highly gratified.*]

I had barely entered the gardens again, when I was seen again, and this time, they chased me half the way to Florence. It was dawn, before I was free of them.

THE DUCHESS

[*Grudgingly.*]

Benvenuto, I may have been hasty. But you do not know of the night I spent. . . . First, there was the Duke, on the balcony. I thought you hidden behind my door, and dared not return to my room. The

Duke, who never takes the night air, this time took it into his head to stand and stand and stand. . .

CELLINI

That must have been irritating.

THE DUCHESS

He had the funniest look on his face: I was afraid that he knew you had been with me. . . Finally, I managed to see that you weren't behind the door, and retired to my room. . .

CELLINI

But not alone, for my thoughts followed you there!

THE DUCHESS

[*Smilingly—at last!*]
Then they went too far! . . . I waited forever, it seemed, and went out on the terrace again. You were nowhere in sight. . .

CELLINI

No, Madam, I was not!

THE DUCHESS

I walked around the corner of the terrace, and saw a man, and thought it was you. . .

CELLINI

Probably at the very moment I was choking the fellow who had caught me!

THE DUCHESS

It was the Duke, in his nightgown, peering into the darkness as if looking for someone! He professed to have been sleep-walking, but I saw that he was lying. I retired to my room, fearing one instant that you would come, and the next, that you wouldn't.

CELLINI

My Lady——

THE DUCHESS

You offend me again. Your manner of addressing me, does. I have instructed you not to call me Your Lady!

CELLINI

[*Attempting to clasp victory in his arms.*]
My Love!

THE DUCHESS

[*Waving him away.*]
Do not make love to me.

CELLINI

Beauty's mother, I said, was cruelty.

THE DUCHESS

Poets rarely forget their own lines. Benvenuto,
I will be frank with you. I do not believe your story.

CELLINI

[*Taken aback.*]
But surely——

THE DUCHESS

There were queer doings at the Palace, last night,
and I know only a part of what happened. Something
happened—I caught the smell of it in my husband's
perambulations, in your running away, in the very
air!

CELLINI

I did not run away—I was chased away. What
can I say if you will not believe me?

THE DUCHESS

I did not say that. I said, I *do* not believe you!
But I *will* believe you, although I do not; for there
are fables which our hearts accept while our minds
reject them. Your fable is one of those.

CELLINI

I ask no more than that your heart believe me.

THE DUCHESS

It does, Benvenuto—but stay, keep your distance;
yet: I would warn you, first, that the credulity of

even my heart can be taxed too far! Look to it, in the future, my friend, that you do not vanish from my threshold into the wide, dark world!

CELLINI

My desire has never left your threshold.

THE DUCHESS

[*Producing her key from her bosom.*]
It cannot cross my threshold without this. . . .
   [CELLINI's *hand stretches forth hopefully; as it
     does, a terrific pounding shakes the rear
     door.*]

OTTAVIANO'S VOICE

[*Outside.*]
Open the door, or we break it down!

THE DUCHESS

[*Returning her key to her bosom.*]
It is Ottaviano!
   [BEATRICE *enters left front.*]

BEATRICE

[*Jubilantly.*]
They've come to hang Cellini!
   [*A crash against the door shows that Ottavi-
     ano is making good his threat.* BEATRICE
     rushes to the door and swings the bolt.* CEL-
     LINI, *with drawn sword, stands ready; the*

Duchess *goes to the extreme right front.*
Ottaviano *and his* Soldiers *burst in with*
bared weapons; behind them, the Hangman,
a frightful individual, rope in hand.]

OTTAVIANO

[*Taking in* Cellini *at first glance, but missing*
the Duchess.]
There he is!—Cellini, you are under arrest.

CELLINI

Not yet.
[Pier *enters left front, followed by several*
Soldiers, *who have come through the house,*
and now stand guard at the exit.]

OTTAVIANO

Resistance is useless. You are outnumbered.

CELLINI

I am never outnumbered while my sword is in my
hand.

OTTAVIANO

[*Contemptuously.*]
More histrionics. [*To his* Soldiers.] Seize him,
but don't hurt him.

THE DUCHESS

[*Going down center.*]

Ottaviano, I forbid it!
[*The* SOLDIERS *pause uncertainly.*]

OTTAVIANO

[*Displeased by her presence.*]
My Lady, I did not see you.

THE DUCHESS

[*Imperiously.*]
I forbid it, I say.

OTTAVIANO

[*Rudely.*]
Madam, keep away.   This is man's work.

THE DUCHESS

[*Angered.*]
I notice that you take no part in it.

OTTAVIANO

Madam, you interfere with the Duke's orders. [*To his* SOLDIERS.] Don't stand like clowns! Seize him, I said. [*The* SOLDIERS *close in on* CELLINI. *The swords flash brilliantly.* PIER *prevents the two guardsmen at the left front door from joining their companions by engaging them himself. One of the attackers mounts the table and jumps on* CELLINI'S *shoulders, bearing him to the ground, where he is disarmed.* OTTAVIANO *turns to see* PIER *still fighting valiantly.*]   Arrest that fool!

[PIER *is pinioned from behind and relieved of his weapon.* CELLINI *is brought down center stage.* BEATRICE, *who has cowered left rear while the battle was on, approaches the crowd.*]

BEATRICE

[*Plucking* OTTAVIANO *by the sleeve.*]

O noble Sir! A good day's work! He don't pay his honest debts.

[OTTAVIANO *hurls her from him.*]

THE DUCHESS

[*Going center stage herself, and not concealing her rage.*]

And having insulted me, what do you intend to do further?

OTTAVIANO

[*Diplomatically.*]

Madam, there was no insult intended. I only obey the Duke's orders to hang Cellini as soon as he is caught. I propose to do this—at once.

THE DUCHESS

Do you presume that your own will supersedes mine?

OTTAVIANO

Madam, I presume that the Duke's will supersedes all others.

THE DUCHESS

What is the charge against Cellini?

OTTAVIANO

Didn't Alessandro tell you?

THE DUCHESS

Alessandro acted at breakfast as if he had lost his Dukedom. He said nothing.

OTTAVIANO

Perhaps he mourned that one of his subjects should be so faithless as to plot against his life.

THE DUCHESS

Cellini?

OTTAVIANO

Cellini, Madam, and in pursuit or his murderous aim, he went last night to the Summer Palace.

THE DUCHESS

[*Imprudently.*]
That is not true.

OTTAVIANO

[*Stiffening.*]
Have you any proof, Madam?

THE DUCHESS

[*Quickly.*]
No. Who discovered this plot of Cellini's?

OTTAVIANO

[*Impatiently.*]
Madam, for some reason you parley for time.

THE DUCHESS

[*Arrogantly.*]
Who discovered this plot?

OTTAVIANO

[*With bad grace.*]
I did, Madam.

THE DUCHESS

[*To* CELLINI.]
Is this true?

CELLINI

[*Putting all of his despair into two words.*]
He lies.

THE DUCHESS

[*Facing* OTTAVIANO.]
I know: it is one of his oldest habits.

OTTAVIANO

[*Venting his rage on the* HANGMAN.]
Why don't you get to work?

THE DUCHESS

[*As the* HANGMAN *adjusts the rope around* CELLIINI's *neck.*]

If you hang him now, I will assuredly hang you tomorrow.

[*The* HANGMAN *pauses, looks at* OTTAVIANO.]

OTTAVIANO

If you don't hang him now, I will assuredly hang you today.

THE HANGMAN

[*With a hoarse laugh.*]

My Lady, I had rather it was tomorrow.

[CELLINI *is hoisted on a chair.*]

OTTAVIANO

[*Triumphantly.*]

Cellini, your time has come.

[*A fanfare of trumpets outside.*]

THE DUCHESS

[*Triumphantly.*]

Cellini, your time has not come.

BEATRICE

[*At the rear door.*]

It's the Duke! I see his gentlemen.

OTTAVIANO

[*Calmly.*]

He will be in time for the execution, Madam.

[*Enter the* DUKE, *his courtiers, and trailing a few feet behind,* EMILIA.]

THE DUKE

[*Surveying the situation.*]

How fortunate! I was afraid that I might be late
for the happy event. [*Sees the* DUCHESS.] What
Madam, you too? We shall both see it, then.

THE DUCHESS

I hope not, Alessandro.

THE DUKE

Your feelings are too tender. A ruler should
cultivate firmness. [*To* OTTAVIANO.] Can he be
hanged here?

OTTAVIANO

[*Points to the ceiling.*]

Those rafters will do excellently.

THE DUKE

[*Looking up.*]

So they will. Probably put there for that very
purpose. Will someone bring me a stool? [*A courtier places two chairs side by side. The* DUKE, *to
the* DUCHESS.] Madam?

THE DUCHESS

[*Her foot beating a tattoo.*]

I will stand, My Lord.

THE DUKE

What are you angry about, Madam?

THE DUCHESS

I am not angry—yet, My Lord.

THE DUKE

You're always angry when your foot goes that way! [*Looks at the chairs, seats himself.*]   Well, as you please, Madam.   And now, let us proceed with our business.

THE DUCHESS

Alessandro.

THE DUKE

One moment, my dear! I want to see that everything is done properly. Has Cellini been introduced to the gentleman who hangs him?

CELLINI

My acquaintance with him is sufficient, My Lord.

THE DUKE

[*Applauding.*]
Bravo, Cellini! An excellent spirit. It's a pity you plotted against me.

CELLINI

[*Passionately.*]
My Lord, I never did!

THE DUCHESS

[*In the same breath.*]
My Lord, he never did!

THE DUKE

What's this? What's this? [*To* OTTAVIANO.]
He says that he never did.

[*The* HANGMAN *climbs up to one of the rafters
with the loose end of the rope.*]

OTTAVIANO

He still hopes for life, Alessandro.

THE DUKE

That's absurd. He hasn't a chance.

[ASCANIO, *affrighted by the scene which greets
him, enters cautiously and creeps to the rear,
where he discovers* EMILIA.]

THE DUCHESS

Alessandro, you must listen to me.

THE DUKE

I am always attentive to what you say.

THE DUCHESS

You must hear Cellini's story.

THE DUKE

Madam, I have no doubt it would be worth hearing—his stories are always interesting; but my mind
is made up.

THE DUCHESS

[*Her foot tapping.*]
You must hear him.

THE DUKE

[*Trying to look firm.*]
You're too tender-hearted. . . . I wish you wouldn't do that with your foot; it makes me nervous.

THE DUCHESS

Did you not hear me say that you must listen to Cellini?

THE DUKE

[*Pleadingly.*]
My dear, he simply must be executed. I've been looking forward to it all morning.

OTTAVIANO

Madam, your concern is unnecessary. He dies justly.

CELLINI

[*Trying to get at him.*]
Liar! Hypocrite! Assassin!

THE DUKE

[*To his wife.*]
There! You see the sort of things he says. I won't hear another word.

THE DUCHESS

[*To* CELLINI.]

My Lord is anxious to hear your story. Tell him what you have to say.

THE DUKE

Oh, well, all right! I'll listen until things are ready.

CELLINI

My Lord, it was Ottaviano——

OTTAVIANO

[*Loudly, to the* HANGMAN *on the rafters.*]

Don't take an age to finish that!

THE DUKE

[*To* OTTAVIANO.]

Not so much noise—I can't hear him.

THE DUCHESS

Perhaps he does not want you to hear him, Alessandro.

CELLINI

My Lord, he does not, for he knows that before I am through, it is he that will be in this halter.

THE DUCHESS

[*Quickly.*]

You accuse him?

OTTAVIANO

[*To the* HANGMAN.]
Ready?

THE DUKE

[*To* CELLINI.]
You accuse Ottaviano?

THE HANGMAN

[*Calling down.*]
Ready.

CELLINI

I accuse Ottaviano!

OTTAVIANO

Everything is ready, Alessandro.

THE DUCHESS

Everything but justice, perhaps.

THE DUKE

[*Peevishly, to* OTTAVIANO.]
Don't rush me. There's plenty of time to hang him.

OTTAVIANO

I protest, My Lord. He will say anything of anybody for a few more moments of breath.

THE DUKE

Will it do any harm to let him waste his breath before he loses it? [*To* CELLINI.] Proceed.

CELLINI

My Lord, yesterday you left Ottaviano behind in this room.

THE DUKE

I don't recall, but I probably did.

CELLINI

He proposed to me that it would be to our advantage if you were put out of the way.

OTTAVIANO

Ridiculous!

THE DUKE

[*Angrily.*]

I don't think it ridiculous that I should be put out of the way. [*To* CELLINI.] But Ottaviano told me last night that it was you who had suggested the idea.

THE DUCHESS

Perhaps to protect himself.

CELLINI

Precisely, Madam. [*To the* DUKE.] My one thought was to tell of the plot. But how could I reach you? I was guarded. I told the soldier I must see you, and he laughed at me. There was nothing left to do but kill him.

THE DUKE

Of course.

CELLINI

Then I went to the Summer Palace, for no other reason than to see you.

THE DUKE

But why did you not ask for me at the Palace?

CELLINI

Because I stumbled across Polverino, and had to kill him.

THE DUKE

[*In a tone of reproach.*]
I don't think that was necessary.

CELLINI

He attacked me. When I saw him on the ground, I lost my head and ran away.

THE DUCHESS

[*To the* DUKE.]
Don't you see? Ottaviano, finding that Cellini had fled, suspected that he was on his way to tell you. . . .

CELLINI

And laid the plot to me!

THE DUKE

[*To* OTTAVIANO.]
What do you say to all this?

OTTAVIANO

It needs no explanation. Here is a man about to swing. He tries to save his neck at the expense of mine.

THE DUKE

[*To the* DUCHESS.]
That sounds reasonable. It's what I would do. [*She shakes her head negatively.*] Oh! No?

CELLINI

My Lord, if I were the guilty one, why did I send word of my whereabouts?

THE DUKE

[*To* OTTAVIANO.]
He scored there.

OTTAVIANO

[*Indignantly.*]
Will you take the word of this cutthroat against my word?

THE DUKE

[*Apologetically.*]
Don't think that of me. I'm just listening to him to please my wife.

THE DUCHESS

[*To the* DUKE.]
Have you forgotten what happened three years ago?

THE DUKE

Of course I have; you know very well I can't remember five minutes back.

OTTAVIANO

[*Haughtily.*]

My Lord, I am a Medici, and I claim the right of protection from further insult. My honor is at stake; you must hang Cellini, or you must hang me. In the name of our family, I demand, which of us will you hang?

THE DUKE

Cellini, naturally . . . but still . . .

OTTAVIANO

Let him produce a witness to his story.

THE DUKE

[*To* CELLINI.]

Can you?

CELLINI

We were alone, My Lord.

THE DUKE

You should always have a witness. They often come in handy.

[ASCANIO, *who has gradually forged to the*

front during the argument, now throws him-
self at the DUKE's *feet.*]
Hello! What do you want?

ASCANIO

[*Stammering in fright.*]
My Lord, I heard them.

THE DUKE

[*To* CELLINI.]
I thought you had no witness.

CELLINI

[*Astonished.*]
I thought we were alone, My Lord.

THE DUKE

[*To* ASCANIO.]
He thought they were alone. Where were you?

ASCANIO

[*Indicating.*]
Under the workbench, My Lord.

THE DUKE

[*To* ASCANIO.]
Under the workbench? That's no place to be.

ASCANIO

I was afraid of a beating, My Lord.

THE DUCHESS

Ah! So you hid there?

ASCANIO

Yes, My Lady.

THE DUKE

And what happened?

ASCANIO

The Master and . . . the other one, came in. The other one wanted the Master to kill you.

THE DUKE

Which other one?

ASCANIO

[*Pointing to* OTTAVIANO.]
That one . .

OTTAVIANO

The boy lies.

THE DUKE

It's not the other one, then, but that one. Well, what happened?

ASCANIO

The Master would not do it.

OTTAVIANO

The boy lies.

THE DUKE

[*To* OTTAVIANO.]
Where's your witness?

OTTAVIANO

I have none. I need none.

THE DUKE

You never can tell; this one was hidden under the table; did you have a look in the furnace?

OTTAVIANO

The boy lies.

CELLINI

Ascanio speaks the truth.

OTTAVIANO

He lies, I say! He is faithful to his master and has invented this yarn to save him.

THE DUKE

Very likely you're right . . . but it does seem convincing.

THE DUCHESS

[*To* ASCANIO.]
What else did Ottaviano say?

ASCANIO

[*Blubbering.*]
I don't know if I should tell, My Lady.

THE DUCHESS

You need not be afraid. Speak.

ASCANIO

He said that the Duke is an ass.

THE DUKE

[*Very angry.*]
Did he say that? Then I'll hang him in Cellini's place.

OTTAVIANO

I never said that you were an ass, Alessandro.

THE DUKE

I should hope not: I was always considered the bright boy of the family! Pier! Where's Pier? [*Sees that* PIER *is held by two guardsmen.*] Release him! [PIER, *free, steps to the* DUKE.] Pier, you knew my father. Didn't he consider me a wit? Wasn't he always laughing at me?

PIER

He was, My Lord.

OTTAVIANO

My Lord, I am a Medici against perjurers! I
never said that you were an ass.

THE DUKE

[*Glowering at him.*]
Maybe not, but it sounds like you to say it.

OTTAVIANO

This rascally boy is Cellini's apprentice; what is
such a witness worth against my word?

THE DUKE

[*Hesitantly.*]
It's a point. I don't know.

THE DUCHESS

[*Ringingly.*]
Then we will call another witness against Ottaviano—no apprentice, but a man, and a Medici!

THE DUKE

Who? Where was he hiding?

THE DUCHESS

I call Ottaviano against Ottaviano. My Lord, I

asked if you remembered what happened three years ago?

THE DUKE

What does it matter, now?

THE DUCHESS

This much: that it convicts Ottaviano!
[*She whispers in the* DUKE's *ear.*]

THE DUKE

[*Starting.*]
And fancy, I forgot. [*To* OTTAVIANO.] You tried to have me killed before.

OTTAVIANO

[*Throwing himself at the* DUKE's *feet.*]
You forgave me, My Lord!

THE DUKE

[*Firmly.*]
You have been at it again.

OTTAVIANO

I swear that I have not.

THE DUKE

I swear that you have . . . and added insult to injury by calling me an ass. [*Throws a purse on*

the floor and turns to the SOLDIERS.] That to the
man who takes the rope from Cellini's neck!

> [*The* SOLDIERS *swarm to* CELLINI *for the re-
> ward.*]

CELLINI

> [*Stepping joyfully from his perch, after rough
> handling.*]

My Lord, you have almost killed me with kindness.

> [*The victor bends for his spoils.*]

THE DUCHESS

> [*Tossing her purse where the other was.*]

That to the man who puts the rope around Ottaviano's neck!

OTTAVIANO

> [*In the halter.*]

I throw myself on your mercy, My Lord.

THE DUKE

I will hang you on the rafter where you would
have hanged Cellini.

THE DUCHESS

> [*Spontaneously.*]

I feel too happy to see even Ottaviano hanged today.

THE DUKE

You are too tender-hearted, my dear, but you shall have your way. [*To the* SOLDIERS.] Lead this fellow forth through the streets of Florence, as an example to all villains, and lodge him in jail. We shall see justice done tomorrow.

OTTAVIANO

[*Struggling.*]
My Lord, forgive me.

THE DUKE

Never.

OTTAVIANO

[*Feeling that he has no more to lose.*]
Then I did say it—you are an ass.
[*He spits at the* DUKE.]

THE DUKE

[*Violently, as* OTTAVIANO *is removed.*]
Put him in a rat-infested cell! Don't be particular about his meals! Don't give him vinegar, he likes it!
[OTTAVIANO *and the* SOLDIERS *are gone. The* HANGMAN *has coiled his rope and descended.*]
[*To him.*]
It's a shame that all your work was wasted: I

know just how you feel. We'll make up for it, to-morrow.

[*The* HANGMAN *exits.*]

THE DUCHESS

[*Severely.*]
Cellini, let this be a lesson to you: never do any-thing which is not open and above board. [*To the* DUKE.] My Lord, you are to be congratulated on your wisdom; a great injustice has been avoided.

THE DUKE

I think myself I handled it rather well.

THE DUCHESS

But I had no intention of staying here, this length of time! I must go.

THE DUKE

[*Surprised.*]
You came unescorted? Will you have a gentle-man?

THE DUCHESS

I brought a page with me; he awaits outside. Cellini, I shall want you to decorate the fountain at the Palace.

CELLINI

My Lady, your service is my pleasure.

THE DUKE

[*Beaming.*]
Very prettily put.

THE DUCHESS

My Lord, gentlemen, I wish you good-morning.
[*To* CELLINI.]   I shall let you know further. . . .
[*Obeisances on all sides, as she goes.*]

CELLINI

[*Dropping to his knees.*]
My Lord, you have given me my life.

THE DUKE

[*Patting him.*]
A poor gift, in itself; you shall make the dies of
my mint, as well.

CELLINI

[*After kissing the* DUKE'S *hand.*]
My Lord, here is a miracle: that I, a poor sculptor, can repay a Prince's generosity—with more than
its equal. I have a gift for you.

THE DUKE

[*Frowning.*]
What is this gift that you have?

CELLINI

A jewel, my Lord.

THE DUKE

[*His frown deepening.*]
I have many jewels.

CELLINI

My Lord, you have no jewels unless you have this jewel.

THE DUKE

Let me see it.

CELLINI

But not, My Lord, with the world at your back. Your Excellency's eyes should feast alone.

THE DUKE

[*To his courtiers.*]
Gentlemen, I will see this mysterious gift. You will await me outside. [*They exit rear. The* DUKE *notices* BEATRICE.] What, old goat-face? Still alive? How disappointing!

[CELLINI *darts a look at* BEATRICE *which sends her out left rear, but she looks in curiously, now and again.* . . EMILIA *and* ASCANIO *exit.*]

CELLINI

My Lord, be prepared for eternal beauty, which

never existed before this age, and which must per-
ish with it.   [*He goes to the right front exit and
calls.*]   Angela!

THE DUKE

[*Rising with delight.*]
Angela?   Here?
[ANGELA *appears at the right front entrance.*]

ANGELA

[*Reproachfully, to* CELLINI.]
You made me wait for the longest time!

THE DUKE

Angela.

ANGELA

My Lord!

THE DUKE

[*With a change of countenance, to* CELLINI.]
What's she doing here?

CELLINI

My Lord, I found her wandering in the gardens,
fearful of the Duchess.   There was nothing to do
but bring her with me.

THE DUKE

[*To* ANGELA.]
If you knew the night I'd spent!   Peering into
dark corners, thinking you were hidden there. . .

CELLINI

My Lord, I love this girl.

THE DUKE

I fancied yesterday you were sweet on her.

CELLINI

I love her, with all my heart and soul. Life without her will be arid and desolate. But, My Lord, I must think of your great generosity to me.

THE DUKE

You affect me, Benvenuto.

CELLINI

The house without her will be quiet, My Lord.

THE DUKE

You'll miss her about you?

CELLINI

I will, My Lord. I will wonder why she is not near me, when I work, and I will long for her gay little chatter! But I must think of your great generosity to me.

THE DUKE

I am moved, Benvenuto.

CELLINI

My Lord, I boasted that I would give you a gift as precious as the one you gave me. You gave me life, and in return, I give you the life of my life.

THE DUKE

[*Exploding.*]
Damn it! I won't let you do it!

CELLINI

My duty to you comes before my happiness, My Lord. Take her and leave me to the stillness of my house.

THE DUKE

Benvenuto, we are both men of sentiment. I can't let you sacrifice your happiness for mine.

CELLINI

My Lord, I will get along somehow, without her.

THE DUKE

You have given her to me, nobly, and I give her back to you.

CELLINI

[*Panic-stricken.*]
You will offend me deeply, My Lord. My Lord, I will learn not to miss her, on my word. Time heals the bitterest hurt.

ANGELA

[*Who has listened mutely, goes to the* DUKE.]
My Lord, take me with you.

THE DUKE

[*Pleased.*]
What do you think of that! She wants to come
with me.

ANGELA

[*Without malice.*]
He doesn't want me.

THE DUKE

You shouldn't say that; he was doing a very fine
thing. [*Idly slips an arm around her.*] You *are*
a lovely thing!

CELLINI

My Lord, I cannot bear this. Take her, I implore
you.

THE DUKE

[*Clearing his throat.*]
You really think that you could do without her?

CELLINI

My Lord, I am sure of it.

THE DUKE

And . . . her absence would not have a perma-
nent effect?

CELLINI

My Lord, it would sweeten my nature.

THE DUKE

Then Benvenuto, I will not offend you: I will take her.

ANGELA

My Lord, I go with you willingly.   But you must promise me one thing.

THE DUKE

You can have all of Florence.

ANGELA

I want my mother sent out of the country.

THE DUKE

Nothing could give me more pleasure.   [*To* CELLINI.]   You shall see Angela as long as possible.   I insist that you walk to the gate with us.

CELLINI

My Lord, you are as tactful as you are wise.
    [*They exit rear.*   EMILIA *runs in, pursued by* ASCANIO; *he corners her.*]

EMILIA

Alligator!   Crocodile!   Vermin!

ASCANIO

[*Pleadingly.*]
I followed you all the way to the Summer Palace
and couldn't find you.

EMILIA

You had no right! . . . I wouldn't have seen you.
If I had . . .

ASCANIO

[*Closing in on her.*]
You can't get away from me, now.

EMILIA

[*As he forcefully embraces her, yields herself
    completely.*]
Oh, my darling Ascanio!

ASCANIO

[*Amazed.*]
You love me?

EMILIA

[*Sobbing.*]
Terribly.

ASCANIO

I thought you hated me. [*Exultantly.*] I'm
going to have you.

EMILIA

I know it . . . but be good to me, be good to me.
[CELLINI *enters and grabs* ASCANIO *by the collar.*]

CELLINI

What the devil do you mean by listening to my
private conversations?
[*Sends him spinning.*]

ASCANIO

[*Clutching* EMILIA's *hand.*]
I know a place where we can be alone.
[*They run out.* CELLINI *returns to the anvil.*
BEATRICE *appears at the right rear.*]

BEATRICE

[*Jeeringly.*]
Wouldn't give me my money, and now the Duke's
got her! What's your forty ducats? I'll live in
Florence like a Queen!
[CELLINI *throws the hammer at her; she ducks
and disappears just as a* PAGE *enters.*]

THE PAGE

[*Inquisitively.*]
I was told to ask for Cellini.

CELLINI

What have you?

THE PAGE

[*Producing the* DUCHESS's *key.*]
My Lady wants you to make a duplicate of this.

CELLINI

[*Taking the key.*]
Tell her she shall have it tonight.
[*Once more, he gazes at the key.*]

THE END

www.ingramcontent.com/pod-product-compliance
Lightning Source LLC
Chambersburg PA
CBHW031405250626
47155CB00004B/1417